Roswell Rice

An Oration on Messiah's Kingdom and Descant on Time and

Immortality

With a Variety of Poetry on Moral and Religious Subjects. Volume for 1875

Roswell Rice

An Oration on Messiah's Kingdom and Descant on Time and Immortality
With a Variety of Poetry on Moral and Religious Subjects. Volume for 1875

ISBN/EAN: 9783337171223

Printed in Europe, USA, Canada, Australia, Japan

Cover: Foto ©Andreas Hilbeck / pixelio.de

More available books at **www.hansebooks.com**

AN ORATION

ON

Messiah's Kingdom,

AND

DESCANT ON TIME AND IMMORTALITY,

WITH A VARIETY OF POETRY ON MORAL AND RELIGIOUS
SUBJECTS.

BY

ROSWELL RICE, Esq.,

of Cambridge, Washington County, N. Y.

PRICE FIFTY CENTS.

VOLUME FOR 1875.

ALBANY:

MUNSELL, PRINTER, 82 STATE STREET.

1874.

INDEX.

N. B.— This Pamphlet of 128 pages was never excelled by an American Author on the subjects of the above Index. The assertion is bold! but the work proves it true. Let the reader judge for himself; and not be led astray by the vain opinions of men; for such is too often the practice of our apostate world.

FERGUSON ALBANY

ORATION IX.

MESSIAH'S KINGDOM.

An *Extract* from the *Works* of *Nature*, *"God manifest* in the *Flesh,"* and the *Wisdom* of *Men*.

God, in his majesty, stretched forth his arm and made the world, the air, the water, and dry land. All things created sprang from his omnific word. He made the sun a light by day, the moon by night, and stars that glitter in their sockets like sparkling gems of silver. He made the herb of the field, and every green thing; the river and ocean, the hill and dale, the feathered songsters to chant his praise, and the countless millions of finny tribes, which tell as living witnesses of his creative power, and dumbly set forth the glory of his omnipotence.

After which, God created man in his own image; pronounced his benediction upon him; made him ruler over fish, fowl, beast and bird, and every living thing that creepeth, or on the earth doth move.

Now God created man, male and female; prepared an Eden for their souls' delight; commissioned them to eat of all the fruit of the garden, except the forbidden "tree of good and evil," on which was stamped the penalty of death. But how short their glory! How soon the death-knell tolled their sad mortality, and sapient angels dropped their silent tears, put on their robes of mourning, and stood confounded at the strange imbecility of man. The Prince of Darkness, foe to all goodness, beguiled the woman; "she plucked, she ate;" at that moment the loud acclamations of hell were heard through its black domains, while heaven let fall a tear. The woman beguiled the man; he also partook of the forbidden tree, thereby incurred the curse of God's

interdiction, drove back the chariot of his Father's
love, and bound himself and his offspring in the dark
dominions of death and hell.   In that dread moment
all was lost!   Earth felt her chains, heaved to her centre,
and in pangs expired.

Man, in his dread dilemma, cursed of his God, and
driven from the garden by the avenging sword guarding
the forbidden tree, becomes a sad vagrant in his ruined
state, sees no star to illume his darkness, no aid to cheer
his fallen soul.   The curse of a broken law remains
upon him; "he is covered with wounds and bruises,"
and the fires of Mount Sinai make his soul to quake
with fear.   He looks back, and his load of guilt over-
shadows him; before him is death temporal and eternal,
and no created arm can save him from the fall.   He has
lost his Eden, the favor of his Lord, and must swell the
sad dirge of his temporal and eternal pain.   O God!
Is this man's doom by heaven's divine decree?

But, lo!   I hear the ministration of the angel band.
The morning stars begin their song of deliverance, and
bring hope to man.   The sapient conclave of the Father,
Son, and Holy Ghost, have found a scheme for a lost
world's redemption, and the sweet harbingers of heaven
begin to proclaim their anthems of deliverance from the
tops of the holy mountains: "The seed of the woman
shall bruise the serpent's head;" "Jehovah shall be
clothed incarnate;" "God shall be manifest in the flesh,
seen of angels, believed on by the world, and re-ascend
into glory; shall tread the wine-press alone, dip his
vesture in his own blood, be buffeted in the streets of
the Jews, and bear the cross up Mount Calvary."   And
all this for who?   For the vile offender, the miscreant
against God's law, for all Adam's lost sons and daughters.
Wonder, O heavens! and be astonished, O earth! at
this boundless love of God to man.

No blood of beasts, or sprinkling priest, can make
reconciliation between Jehovah and a lost world.   Nothing, but God the Son, clothed in his humanity, can
make an atonement for the sinner's soul, save him from

impending wrath, and restore him to his lost Eden. Therefore, the second person in the Trinity leaves the abode of the heavenly hosts, casts off his diadem, fulfills the prophecy, is born in a stable and cradled in a manger; the son of Mary, and Son of God. This is the love of Jesus for us, the hope of our redemption. Wonder, O my soul! for the Lord has promised to ransom mankind, when he shall give up his life on Calvary.

We now approach the scene of a Savior's sufferings to restore a lost world. See him across the Kidron stream, forsaken by his disciples, his Father's countenance withdrawn, divinity receding from suffering humanity, in the dire scene of unparalleled agony, when God's wrath, for sin, fell on the shoulders of our surety, our only hope. Here, in his midnight conflict with heaven, earth and hell, "it pleased Jehovah to bruise him." "God spared not his own Son." "The chastisement of our peace was upon him." "By his stripes we are healed." Three times, in Gethsemane, shrinking humanity deprecated the cup. Three times he prostrated himself in prayer to his Father; and three times he arose in the conflict, resolved to reach the goal of his sufferings. O God! what power stayed thy arm in thy Son's mortal agony!

To describe the scene, the utmost powers of conception fail. We but approach the verge of the tragedy. What pen can tell the anguish of his heart, or exhibit its bruised emotions? The alternative was before him. If he failed to die, his Father, of Adam's progeny, would feed the flames of hell! Millions upon millions must tread the road to perdition, and the blighting curse of God, unreconciled, set in upon them forever! Satan would shout in victory, and boast in his bound confederates! Heaven would be lost, and the prospective thrones of eternity exchanged for chains of perdition. The untrodden wine-press was before him! The hour of almighty conflict had arrived! The devotees of sin were about him, and heaven's squadrons above, but none to help. Therefore, by his own might, he drank the cup alone, mingled with dregs of death and hell!

The design of the Savior's sufferings connects itself with the history of his propitiation. The effect, the end, explain the cause producing the result. The circumstances attending his death prove it the most momentous event that ever occurred in the history of man. Prophets, apostles, heroes, and martyrs have been burned, banished, stoned, and sawed asunder; myriads have died in battle; pestilence, with putrefactive breath, has inspired the lungs of pallid millions; thrones, in a night, have been destroyed; but no event on the records of history has been so attested by nature and nature's God, as the death of Christ. This proves the dignity of the sufferer, and the divine grandeur of the sacrifice.

Six days before his death, he makes it known to his disciples! He announces his resurrection! after which, he agrees to meet his brethren in a mountain of Galilee. He is arrested and brought before Annas, Caiaphas, Herod, and Pilate; proved guilty by false witnesses, and sentenced to an execution, more infamous and painful in its nature, than any in the code of nations. In the hall he is scourged, buffeted, and spit upon, mocked, crowned with thorns, and sceptred with a reed. From the pavement of Pilate, he bears his cross through the streets of the Jews. He faints under his load, "and they compel a Cyrenian to bear the cross" up the hill "with Jesus." Thus he was sentenced by man, and by him crucified and slain.

Here we pause. Was the compulsion ever regretted by the Cyrenian in bearing the cross? and did the daughter of Paganism, the wife of Pilate, lament that she sought the salvation of Jesus, in urging her husband to have nothing to do "with that just person?" And when she died, was her plea for the God-man left unrewarded? But he heeds not her prayer. The reprobate mob, and mass of Jewish spectators shout, "his blood be on us, and on our children;" invoking his curse by the foulest envy. O God! in what woe shall the future tell the consummation of their chosen anathema! what numbers measure their guilt! what pencil paint their doom.

Again we pause, and view another shade in the picture. A few Christian daughters gaze on their Master, and bewail his anguish. Thank God, this little band could not riot in his torture. Jesus, ever mindful of goodness, with eyes sinking in death, cast a look of godlike philanthropy, and exclaimed, "Daughters of Jerusalem, weep not for me, but for yourselves, and for your children." This city, in which I am judged unfit to live or die, before this generation pass, shall be drenched in blood! Before two years expire, Caiaphas, the stern bigot, shall wind up his career in suicide and death! In the mean time, the treacherous Pilate, in the same manner, shall die by his own hands! Soon, Herod, in his malice, shall be smitten of God, and eaten up of worms! The land of Judea shall be without altar, or temple, and even the Holy of Holics shall fall beneath the Roman's spear! The Sanhedrim, with the multitude of Jews, who raised their voices from a thousand quarters with the cry of crucifixion, shall be crucified, until there shall not be room in the suburbs of Jerusalem to build their crosses; for the vengeance of Rome shall be glutted by every where exhibiting to the lost Jew a surrounding horizon of crucified sufferers. My God! save us from the curse of this unparalleled doom!

For this *Deicide*, this crime unequaled in the history of worlds, the Jews, branded and scorned, shall be scattered in every quarter of the globe, without synagogue or temple, while millions shall perish in their contest with the Gentiles. For this crime, the unerring prophecy has fallen upon them like thunder-bolts from heaven. More than a million * * * fell in the Roman conflict; and, without glancing at the future, near two thousand years have swept in darkness over their desolate pomp and curse-bowed grandeur. No

longer beloved of God, deistical in faith, they roam
without shrine or priest. The four quarters of the
globe confirm their dispersion, and seal their infamy.
The page of history is stained with their blood, and
the winds of heaven bear to insulted majesty the story
of their wrongs, and record of their sighs!

We now approach the final sufferings of the Son of
God! We stand at the base of Calvary! The clam-
orous multitude surround the cross, that their eyes may
drink the blood, and their ears the last groans of murdered innocence! The cross is now prepared! The
suffering victim is stretched upon it! His hands and
feet receive their position! and the stern executioner,
with his ponderous hammer and rugged spikes, is in
haste to give the blow, that nails to the fatal wood the
sacred humanity of the Son of God! The cross is
reared, and by a fearful concussion it enters the mortised
rock. O God! what an appeal this distension must
have been to the suffering Redeemer, tearing the nerves,
muscles, and tendons of his hands and feet, and sending
sick convulsions to his heart. Well might the prophet
exclaim of his sufferings, "no man hath sorrows like
unto *my* sorrows."

In this deed of more than hellish venture, the ruthless soldiery, and heartless mob, led by the chief priests,
scribes, and elders, all united; even one of the thieves,
suspended his death-sobs to revile him, while the shoutings and rejoicings of hell's votaries shook the base of
the mountain: "If thou be the Son of God, come down
from the cross, and we will believe." Eternal justice,
where was thy wrath? Angel of God, where slept thy
sword, and by what arm restrained?

But we live again when we reflect, on that engine of
death bleeds a Victim, whose ransom shall tell on the
world's destiny through the ages of time, and be a ral-
lying point of interest among all the worlds of God.
Though the multitude about him now conspire to bow
the knee in mock prostration, and invite him down from
the cross, "he saved others, let him save himself!"

here hangs the christian's hope, bequeathed by the life-blood of the Man of Calvary.

But the scene changes. Jesus discharges the duties of a son to her, who was identified with him in the scenes of Bethlehem, and story of the manger. He prays for his murderers, and cries with a loud voice, "My God! my God! why hast thou forsaken me?" That these Pagans and Jews forsake me is not so strange; that men should withdraw their aid, and angels refuse to minister, is what I expected. A faithless world and frowning skies I can endure; but, "my God, my God, why hast *thou* forsaken me!" When did I refuse to force thy claims, and sustain thy rights? When did I fail to publish thy name and relieve the hopeless sufferer? When did the poor, the needy, the halt, and blind, ask of me and did not receive? When did the heart-broken father, the weeping mother, and orphan sisters ask me back their dead, and I did not relume the sightless eye, and pulse the lifeless heart? And is this my recompense? Must I not only bear the malice of the mob, fury of fiends, desertion of the world, and murmurings of the heavens above, but also have mingled in this dreadful cup the hidings of my Father's face? "My God, my God, *why* hast thou forsaken me!"

Now, when his suffering humanity had uttered its last complaint, and was about to receive its final shock; when Heaven and earth conspired to recede from the poor sufferer; when the divine intercourse was checked, and paternal presence withdrawn; when alone, without friend or assistance, he had to contend with the conflicting and scourging elements of the universe ; at this strange phenomenon, nature could no longer endure the dread sufferings of her Creator: she vibrated with conscious horror through all her dominions. The sun, shrouded in darkness, rolled back his chariot from the cursed abode of man; refused to see the Son of Righteousness, from whom he had received his beams, sinking beneath a horizon of darkness, blood, and death! The rocks rent, earth shook, and trembling mountains prolonged the terror of the scene; men scoffed, hell howled, and heaven let fall a tear. Death heard the cry of the world's redemption in his dark dominions, forgot his prey, let fall the chains which bound his prisoners; they started into life, while revengeful creation, mantled with sackcloth, "hung the heavens with the habiliments of mourning!"

And all this for man, for you and me. The human soul was at stake, and by such an altar and such a sacrifice, it is proved to be of more value than the whole amplitude of insentient worlds. That, upon which Heaven has embarked so godlike an expenditure of effort, must possess the true value of the immortal soul!

But, the tragical scene is over; the Almighty's wrath seems subsided; nature has put off her garb of mourning; the sun gilds the world in prior glory; the moon ascends her pathway of stars; the mountains cease to tremble on their deep foundations; mossy graves retain their remaining dead; and creation seems to rest over the Savior's tragedy.

His disciples have now lost their Master, and become the scoff of Jewish murderers. Death, with hands dyed in Heaven's blood, now sways his sceptre over the grave of Jesus, and holds the chains, that bind in the tomb, the humanity of the Son of God' Hell exclaims, in a shout of triumph with her countless millions through all the deep caverns of the damned, "the Prince of Life is slain," while earth's demons conspire in the loud acclamation of "Amen."

The Savior is yet nailed to the cursed wood! His head is bowed in the still slumbers of death! His eyes, once sparkling with life, now sleep in silence! His face, without spot or wrinkle, is cold and lifeless! His feet, that bore salvation, have lost their motion; and his beneficent hands, that relieved suffering humanity, are dead in crucifixion. He now remains a spectacle to angels and men, cold and lifeless on the bloody cross!

But a friend now approaches the body of Jesus.

Joseph of Arimathea, takes him down from the cross, embalms him in spices, and lays him in his own sepulchre, hewn out of a rock. His grave is sealed by Jewish priests, and secured by Roman soldiers. He lies "numbered with transgressors," the pale and pulseless corpse of Joseph's tomb!

What a spectacle was exhibited in this memorable sepulchre. He, who clothed himself with light, and rode in his chariot, borne on the breezes of heaven, was pleased to put on the habiliments of mortality, and press the tomb of the prostrate dead. Who can repeat this truth too often? Who can dwell on this theme too long? He, who sustains the thrones of glory, and gives light to the heavenly host, is now a pale corpse, and chained by the Prince of Darkness. But his Divinity only slumbers to prove the claims of his humanity, when he shall tread upon the neck of his last enemy, and raise the banner of the cross over the combined powers of death and hell: then shall his ruthless foes be put to flight, and the song of free grace, by the blood of Jesus, shall redeem the world.

In this, the hour of thy triumph, O death! never did thy dark realm contain such a prisoner before. Prisoner did I say? No, he was more than conqueror! He arose from his icy bed more mightily than Samson from a transient slumber; broke down the iron bars of death, and razed the strong holds of its dark dominions. And this, O mortals! is our security, our only consolation. Jesus has trod the rugged pathway, and smoothed it for our passport. Jesus, sleeping in the tomb, has brightened the mansion, and left an odor in those beds of dust. The dying Jesus is our sure protection and guide through the territories of the grave. If we believe in him, he will transmit us to heaven when we pass under the curtain of our dissolution; for his voice has declared, "whosoever believeth in me, shall never die." Our exit will terminate our sufferings, and our final groan be our admission to everlasting joy; "for, if Christ be risen. then shall we also be raised." "Now is he risen from the dead, and become the first fruits of them that slept." So, in Christ's resurrection, is the consummation of man's redemption.

Our lost hope in Christ's death, revives in his victory over the tomb. We turn from the dark picture, the garden, cross and grave, to gaze on the renewed splendor of the Prince of Life. When the dawn of the morning broke on the night-watch of the disciples, they felt the whole heaven of their hopes was lost, and the sepulchre of their Master was the grave of immortality. But soon they saw the banner of life waving above the citadel of death, when their Jesus triumphed over his last great enemy. Then our nature took wing, and mounted with him from the tomb. Our faith revives in the retrospect, and the future is full of hope before us. When the "great Captain of our salvation" had met and satisfied the last demands of justice; had entered, as our surety, the dark dominions of the dead; had rendered grateful the retreat of the tomb; had perfumed the grave for the believer, and planted the flower of Heaven's eternal spring in the moss of the dark sepulchre: then, then he rose in grandeur over death's proudest hopes, and in godlike triumph, dragged to his ascending car the captivity of a dying world!

But we turn to another shade in the picture: and we here notice, that the types, shadows, and predictions of the Jewish dispensation, were set forth to show the sufferings, death, and resurrection of the Savior: and now being fulfilled by his victory over the grave, prove, beyond contradiction, that God directed the prophecy. When the victim flamed on the altar, it prefigured the offering of Calvary. When Moses lifted up the serpent, he represented Jesus on the cross. When the prophet smote the rock, it was typical of Christ. When the goat was made an expiatory sacrifice for the congregation, it was done to symbolize him, who "bore our sins upon the tree;" the atoning "Lamb of God, that taketh away the sins of the world." If the paschal blood stayed the drawn sword of the destroying angel, how

much more snall the blood of Christ "our passover slain
for us?"

We see prophecy held the same language, and tra-
vailed on the same immortal theme. This was the spring
of the prophets' action, the goal of their hope, and
recompense of their desire. In their describing the
great sacrifice of the new dispensation, every word broke
with the burden of a special revelation. In whatever
course inspiration threw their vision, they saw the cross,
in triumph, rising upon the broad horizon of humanity,
dissipating the gloom of surrounding millions, and
lighting up with splendor, the baneful valley of the
shadow of death.

In this light our Savior regarded his advent and
crucifixion. It was this sustained him. Look at his
patience and resolution mid the insults of his foes, and
tears of his friends. Even when the former did shout
for his execution, and cried, "not this man, but Barabbas;" and his loved ones, despair-stricken, shed tears
of immortal disappointment, with godlike firmness he
braved the fury, for he had before him the prospect of
his passion. He beheld the period, when all nations
shall load the altar of his crucifixion with the incense
of piety, and celebrate the grandeur of his mission, and
his death!

Having noticed man's creation and fall; the sufferings, death, and resurrection of "God manifest in the
flesh;" I shall now contemplate his own Divinity, Godhead, and reign, by referring to the declarations of
inspired prophets and apostles as positive testimony.

To be able to confide in the high commission of the
Son of God in the uplifting our fallen nature to the
fellowship of divine, we must reason on the subject,
regarding him as the self-existing Almighty, Creator
and Ruler of all; the Sustainer of Heaven's rights, and
at the same time retrieving the guilt of mankind: and
to prove Messiah's claims, we must notice him as do the
scriptures, *in his pre-existing, militant, and glorified*

states. In doing this, the New Testament must furnish a key to unlock the Old.

Without preface, or anticipated contradiction, these holy expositions tell us that "he came down from heaven;" that he is "God over all;" "God manifest in the flesh;" that "he was before Abraham;" had "glory with the Father before the world began;" that "he was sent," "was given," "was made flesh," was "Alpha and Omega," "the first and last;" "was, and is, and is to come;" "the Prince of Life;" "the Lord of glory;" "all things were made by him," and "by him all things exist." Thus, the pre-existence of Jesus Christ is every where expressly assumed in the New Testament; therefore, we cannot fail to give it due prominence, for this is our safety; all is sea beside.

To the same effect of the New, is the language of the Old Testament. Here he is the expressed God of universal dominion. In Genesis, as "the seed of the woman," he should obtain victory over the powers of darkness. As the "seed of Abraham," he was to invest himself with glory in the gate of his enemy. He is Job's "redeeming" God. David calls him "Jehovah," the "King of Sion," and his throne "eternal." Agur styles him "God's Son." Isaiah proclaims him the "mighty God, and everlasting Father;" "Immanuel, God with us;" the "God of hosts, and only Savior." Daniel declares his "kingdom without end." Joel gives him the name of "Jehovah;" and in Malachi he is called "the Lord God of hosts." Here we have a cloud of witnesses, all conspiring in the supreme glory and infinite power of God's Messiah.

In his *militant state* on earth, he gave evidence that he was "God manifest in the flesh." At his baptism on the banks of Jordan, the powers of the world to come vouched to the Divinity of his mission! In the Mount of Temptation, he foiled the sagacity of hell by the defeat of her sovereign! In Cana of Galilee, the elements obeyed his creative mandate, while water, casting off the law of its nature, blushed to wine! On the shore of the Lake Genesareth, "the mother of Peter's wife" was taught that disease and death obey his voice! The stormy sea of Galilee, the surging roll of the agitated Tiberias, felt his presence; and the one was still, while the other became as adamant under his feet! In the forest of Bethesda, more than twenty thousand heard his voice, and hung on his lips in breathless expectation, while beholding the supernatural multiplication of bread and fish in the hands and mouth of the eater. By the wayside, a beggar, in rags and misery, directs his sightless balls to the way his Lord was passing; stretched his palsied hands, and feeling for information, he cries, "Jesus, thou son of David, have mercy on me;" and straightway he chides the curse of nature, by throwing the light of heaven on the opening eyes of the blind-born gazer!

A female invalid "troubled him in the crowd," and restoring virtue ran through all her frame in the contact! His rebuke drove life from the fig tree, and anon it withered away! He said to the damsel, "*Talitha cumi*," and death fled from her bier! He cried, "Lazarus, come forth," and his putrefaction began to tremble with the vital spark, and his pulse of life to beat in the tomb! He commanded demons to "depart," and they fled to rejoin the damned! Confession, from lips of devils, declared him to be the holy one of God! The effulgence of his Deity shone on the Mount of Transfiguration! In the procession that attended him through the cantons of Jewry, those who had never seen, "opened their eyes;" and the first object they saw, was him who gave them sight. None but Jehovah could release the woes of suffering humanity, and burst the chains of the death-bound prisoner, as did Jesus, when he took upon him our nature, and dwelt among the sons of men.

Behold him entering Jerusalem! His disciples shouted him as their God and Redeemer. The throng of spectators rent the skies with their loud acclamations, "Hosanna in the highest." The streets of the Jews, and the bending heavens, resounded with the shouts of the multitude; and had they been silent, the stones beneath their feet would have cried in honor to his grandeur!

Again we look at the closing scene of his eventful life. He met death upon the cross, with no aid from earth, save the tears of his friends, amid the scoff of thousands! and yet there was no defeat in his death. The scenes of the crucifixion confirmed his godhead, and threw "the gazer on his knee." The terrific drapery, which, in that dread hour, was thrown around the theatre of nature, proclaimed his dignity, and the godlike glory of his sacrifice.

The glorified state of the Messiah, which commenced at his resurrection, and was confirmed by his ascension and the descent of the Holy Spirit, includes the range of his administration. His resurrection sealed the Divinity of his mission, when he led captivity captive; spoiled principalities and powers, and fastened to his chariot wheels the conquered millions of death and hell. And when he ascended in his glory through the boundless concave of the heavens, had earth possessed angelic ears, she might have heard his princely heralds surprise the waiting throngs of eternity with the voice of thunder, "Lift up your heads, ye everlasting gates, and let the King of Glory in." Earth might have asked, in the language of prophecy, "Who is the King of Glory?" and heaven have replied, earth has crucified him; "the Lord of Hosts, he is the King of Glory!" Such was the triumph of the Son of God!

Thus, in his pre-existent, militant and glorified states, the Godhead belongs to the Messiah, and all the works of Deity are ascribed to him. He was the appearing Jehovah of the world in the days of Noah; the uncreated acting angel in the Jewish ages; the resident God of the temple, and Supreme Head of the Christian church; reigning and controlling the interest and destinies of the universe, with a sway steady as the flow of time, and lasting as the years of eternity!

We now consider his *humiliation*. He was Lord of

David, yet he became his afflicted "Son." The "root" became the offspring of David, and "the eternal Father the Son given." Temptation and sufferings are the great sources of human misery; and to these our Lord was subject during his ministry on earth. As our Redeemer, he humbled himself; as our God, he burst the bands of the sepulchre, and assumed the glory he possessed "before the world was." Infinite was his humiliation in becoming man, yet greater still in dying for man. But in yielding to a death so painful and ignominious as that of the cross, the wonder is magnified, and as we pause on its horizon, we only repeat, "he humbled himself." Almighty condescension could stoop no lower.

This is the mystery of our faith. The law of heaven seems inverted. The God of angels was comforted in Gethsemane by an angel of God. The Judge of the Universe was arraigned before the bar of Pilate, and compelled to bear the engine of his own death to the place of execution. He, who had received the homage of heaven from everlasting, had his spotless cheek polluted by the lips of hell; those lips that sold him, and sealed the compact of his death! Those hands that built the arches of the heavens, and flung through immensity its wilderness of suns; and those feet that trod the sapphire plains of the celestial world, and had the earth a footstool, were spiked in agony to the cursed wood! His brow, that from eternity shone with immortal majesty, was pierced with a diadem of thorns! He, who led the choir of angels, and tuned their golden harps, was crucified between two thieves! He, who supplies your springs, swells your rivers, and bowls the immeasurable ocean, said, "I thirst," and "they gave him gall to drink!" What a boundless surrender of claim!

He was born in a stable; was driven by Herod into Egypt; was obscurely educated in Galilee; was tempted by the devil; was derided by his kindred; was traduced by the Jews, persecuted by the priesthood, betrayed by his disciples, and crucified by the world! Here is the climax of his glory and humiliation. God of eternity, teach us the import of this trans-human mystery, and in our conscious being, penetrate the springs of devout emotion!

In his *passion*, he drank deep of the cup of sorrow before his exaltation to the throne of hisDivinity. His soul seemed to be engaged in the displeasure of Heaven. Whatever confidence he had in God the Father, it is evident he labored under a suspension of heavenly comfort. The passion was a severe trial of the natural affections and moral virtues of our Lord, together with a fearful amount of penal suffering. It was the hour and power of darkness, arrived in the plenitude of their gloom and last visitation.

During the final engagement, the scales of God's justice seemed to tremble with a fearful equipoise. It was an eventful crisis, because the war comprised infinite elements. The hero of the struggle entered into the breach of a world cursed of God, and the strife of contending destinies shook the pillars on which its amplitude was poised. Universal nature sympathized with the Sufferer, and her avenging administrations rebuked the apathy of earth, as the rocks and mountains conspiring with the mourning heavens, broke their eternal silence to vindicate his claims.

I shall now contemplate Messiah's *reign*. His sceptre comprehends "all power in heaven and in earth;" and his administration is universal. He has a two-fold claim upon the children of the world; he made us, and afterwards redeemed us. As "God over all," his right to rule is inherent in his nature; and he also possesses the same right to his Messiahship by his "obedience unto death;" for which cause he stands as mediator between heaven and earth, administering mercy and justice to the children of men.

The constitution of his kingdom was chartered and confirmed before its actual existence over the face of our world. It was the covenant of redemption first published in Paradise; enlarged upon by Abraham; further unfolded at Sion; announced by prophets, and finally consummated by the advent of the Messiah. This covenant includes the true worshippers of all nations in every age of the world, whether before or since our Lord assumed his humanity.

The Jew, the Gentile, the wide world with its teeming population, infernal agency and degeneracy of its nature, the pride of intellect and turbulence of passion, these are the enemies of Messiah's reign, and every fifty years of his administration, for nearly sixty centuries, has consigned to heaven or hell, from our world alone, some five hundred millions of immortal souls, to live and sing in the one, or sigh and wail in the other! He holds in his hand the weal and woe of his subjects; and from his throne of thrones, he will defend, maintain, and extend his rights. His reign mingles joy and grief, and he imparts, by his mighty scale, his just retribution for good and evil, as determined by the character of his subjects.

The reign of the Messiah spreads over the expanse of immensity, and comprehends the length and breadth of his empire. It goes back to the throne of Jehovah, when the "sons of God first shouted for joy," and embraces every intelligence, form and grade of being; it stretches forward until we are lost in the infinities of the future, and only know that the crowned millions of the blest in the central abodes of Deity, find the glories of eternity magnified by "the Lamb being the light thereof."

The laws of this kingdom are those of the Gospel, and relate principally to the manifestations of the divine nature, the medium and method of acceptance with Heaven; and finally, the laws and rules of morality, which are the great principles in regulating the actions of mankind.

To show the past, present, and future extent of this kingdom, we appeal to history, observation, and analogy. And in appealing to history, we know not where to begin.   Through all ages, what nation, not utterly savage, is not a debtor to the cause we plead ?   Where is it, the lamp of his empire has not been seen penetrating the gloom of nature's night ?   Where is it, that light has not shone in darkness, and gilded the gloom of earth's horizon, to direct her aliens home to God ? Where is it, that salvation's morning has not arisen upon the world, as it first broke upon the shepherds' ear, on the hills of Bethlehem !

Every brief term in the calendar of time is adding some new province to the dominions of the Son of God. Every rising sun that gilds the heavens, brings in some new trophy of his reign.   At every short interval, the recording angel stamps on the ledger of immortality, that the Gospel has conquered another language of the babbling earth, and soon it shall pour its salutary streams of light and life through the channels of every dialect ! East, West, North and South ; through all the zones of earth, the world's moral midnight is struggling for her coming dawn !   Every where, over the vast expanse of nations, light is flashing through the mind, giving direction to the hopes, and shedding its lustre upon the path of humanity.

The vast river of the water of life is rolling in heaven-born grandeur, and will soon flood the world in millennial glory, and bear on its bosom the emporium of God.   The seed of the kingdom, already sown upon the tops of the mountains, shall yield its fruit in succeeding ages, and wave like the cedars of Lebanon, bending by the winds of heaven.   The foundation of the kingdom is already planted in the breasts of millions, and its heavenly breezes are every where inspiring the children of men, and will successively augment in its accumulating triumphs, until "faith" shall become universal, and the world restored to God.

In this way, Christianity shall stain the pride of all human glory ; subdue the world with its vile elements, and on its grave raise the banner of Messiah's kingdom. The Prince of Darkness shall lose his reign on earth, and all men learn to do the will of God. The gilded curse of war shall receive its dishonor in the esteem of nations; and auspicious memory, instead of recounting the vain glory in the battles of slaughtered victims, shall consecrate its hallowed recollections to "peace on earth, and good will to men."

The subjects of this kingdom are the servants of God, flourishing in the "beauties of holiness." They are free volunteers, ready to obey the commands of their Master, and are influenced by the life-giving doctrines of the cross. In numbers, "they shall be as the stars of heaven, and sands upon the sea shore."

Messiah, in his reign, not only saves his people, but destroys his enemies. Look at the past ages of the world's history, and see the Almighty breathing his just imprecations on the children of men. From his lips our first parents received the sentence of death. Because of unbelief, he destroyed the antediluvian world by the flood of his wrath. With fire and brimstone he demolished the cities of the plain, while their devotees of Atheism suffocated in death. The ruins of Egypt, Tyre, Babylon, Nineveh, Jerusalem, and Rome remain, to this day, imperishable memorials of the vengeance of Heaven. Look at the Jews, cursed of God, and trodden beneath the insulting feet of an ungrateful world. Look at "the seven churches of Asia," and the cities in which they were found; see their noiseless streets, hymnless temples, and desolated altars. Look at Herod, Pilate, Julian, and many others who persecuted the church; dark and ghastly are the recollections of their madness.

Look at the insanity of infidelity in the God-rejecting republic of France at the close of the last century. See that powerful, civilized, and lettered nation throwing the gauntlet of defiance at the foot of God's throne, and waving, as the flag of their national distinction, the standard of Atheism before his face! Look at their combined allies, shrewd, artful, and malignant, leagued in the shape of turbulent propagandists, for the extermination of all religion. Look at the prince, subaltern, gazetteer, philosopher, and demagogue, uniting in giving organic structure to impiety; elevating unbelief to the dignity of science, and reducing blasphemy to a trade!

Of Jehovah's retribution, in the progress and sequel of this terrible crusade, we need not describe. The principal actors fell from their skeptic thrones, as if God had withered up their being. The minister of vengeance, with his accusing presence, seems to have blasted their gaze, and they perished before the rebuke of him, in whose eye empire is a speck, and man an atom! All this we have seen, and yet we fear the reckoning is but commenced, and that the future will exact a still more fearful atonement.

All possible means of torture have been wielded to destroy Christianity. The axe, the cross, the stake, the fire, and amphitheatre, these only threw a resplendent halo of glory around the ascending martyr. The fadeless crowns of immortality cheered his vision, and bore him above the waves of Jordan. Every infernal project concerted to extinguish the hopes and being of the true church of Christ, only amplified the sphere, and augmented the number of her triumphs. Such has been the past history of Christendom; and prophecy foretells a corresponding train of events shall appear in the future.

The Gospel is already published in more than two hundred languages of the vocal and reading earth. In almost every nation of our globe, "the Son of Righteousness is" beginning to shine "with healing in his wings." The sons and daughters of Paganism are emerging from darkness into light. The idolater of the Ganges, and the savage of the Pacific; the Tungusian ranger of the torrid zone, and the shivering Icelander, amid his icebergs of eternal frost, have caught the radiance of redemption's star, and with tears of joy are pressing their way to the unfurled banner of Messiah's kingdom.

The imposture of Mecca, whose baptism is blood,

and his eucharist slaughter; and whose gigantic form so long appalled and darkened the eastern world, is fast nodding to its fall; and soon the crescent, no longer beaming upon the standard of bandit legions, shall be seen sinking beneath a horizon of oblivion, blood and death. Instead of Saracen minarets, the banner of the cross shall float on the hill of Calvary, and throw the shadow of its folds over the tomb of the Redeemer, and the homaged birth-scene of the world's redemption.

The great martial struggle we have described, is now in a state of evolution, and in every direction, the advance of the Messiah, resistless as the volitions of Deity, is defacing the kingdom of darkness. At this very hour, disciplined and formidable columns, under the blood-stained flag of the cross, are bearing down with invincible steadiness upon the dominions of sin and death. Christianity, with all its prevailing influence, is every where contesting the human mind, by irresistible appeals to all the principles and passions within the vast vortex of human life, and on which character and destiny are made, to turn for time and eternity.

On the one hand, we see the strong holds of skepticism crumbling beneath the chariot wheels of the Redeemer; and on the other, the church in deep travail to obtain the primitive simplicity of Christianity; that by her pure example, and ardent zeal, she may beat back the waves of darkness, and hasten the universal triumph of Messiah's kingdom, "when a nation shall be born in a day, and all shall know the Lord from the least to the greatest."

Finally: In glancing at the last destiny of the church on earth, whether amid the shock of revolutions, or the bloodless triumphs of Messiah's reign, robed in the majesty of moral dominion, and resplendent in the drapery of celestial beauty, the church is seen passing through successive eras of improvement and perfection, each glowing with increasing splendor, until the bursting echoes of a world redeemed, borne off upon the gale, and brought up upon the breeze, shall revive the

recollection, and realize the burden of the hymn of
Bethlehem ; for the shoutings of the last harvest shall
be the song that sowed the seed, "Glory to God in the
highest !" Thought can go no further ; emotion rise
no higher. It is the last effort of language ; the richest
utterance of earth.

DESCANT ON TIME AND IMMORTALITY.

The Author's Excuse—His Prayer to God—Creation of Worlds—
Of Adam and Eve—Their Fall—The Flood—Destruction of Sodom
and Gomorrah—Of Jerusalem—Bonaparte's Career—The Evils of
War—On Death—The World's Redemption—The Resurrection—The
Day of Judgment—The Woes of Hell, and Bliss of Heaven.

Awake, my soul ! from thy deep slumber rise !
Tune well thy harp, ere thou attempt to sing
Thy Descant grave, on Time's destroying flight ;
And touch the strings of endless weal or woe.
My weakness is extreme ! the dark cloud of
Midnight veils my spirit in mournful tones ;
And this frail barque, stamped with mortality
Because of sin, begins to feel the weight
Of years, and soon must wither for the tomb.
'Tis true the task is much too hard for me ;
Yet I will try this worthy song to sing,
Before my harp by death shall be unstrung ;
And I of Time shall take my last farewell.
　O thou Almighty One ! thou God of light !
Eternity past and future took its
Name from thee ! thou wert the "First and Last" ere
Worlds arose from chaos ; and thou shalt be
Through endless future, called God the Father,
God the Savior, and God the Holy Ghost.
Thou who art the Fountain of life,—Giver
Of ev'ry perfect gift, illuminate
My mind, that I may behold the' things not seen

By mortal sight, and justly expose them
To a world of aliens, by Thee redeemed.
Then shall the lost be better by my birth ;
And for this boon their great Creator praise.
This is my heart's desire ! for this I burn
The midnight oil, and spend my sleepless hours.
Were it not for this, my song would cease,—my
Muse expire,—my pen would fall, and all my
Exertions be for self, and self alone.

Time has its tales, unnumbered in their chain ,
Various as the ocean's waves, from the
Rippling, to the mountain swell that rolls the
Mighty deep ; or sundry winds that blow, from
The gentle zephyrs, to the sweeping flight
Of the hurricane. He utters from his
Countless voices, laden with jubilee
Or woe, which bear on their tones the height and
Depth of earth-born glory, and piercing wails
That shake the world. Where shall I begin my
Song ? how tune my harp ? what string first strike ? to
Tell the wonders of Time's rapid flight, as
He bears his living victims to the tomb ?
Ye holy angels, lend your wings ! and ye
Ministering spirits, servants of the
Living God, touch my heart with a live coal
From Heaven's altar, that I may tell of Time's
Momentous weight, before I tune my harp
To strike the notes of Immortality.

The Author of Time is God. He counted
In his own right way, when he said, "Thus be
Thy circumference, O world ! these are thy
Revolutions :—the one shall be called year,
The other day." Thus our teeming orb counts
Time, since first it flew in its revolving
Sphere. Its motions are complete ; it knows no
Increase, or diminution in its course,
Ever since the sun arose, and changed its
Gloomy curtain for meridian light.

What pow'r is that, which bade such wonders rise ?

What arm from chaotic embryo brought
Forth the planetary worlds,—marked their spheres,—
Their circumscription gave?   What eye measured
Those planets, and saw their revolutions
From the beginning?   Who was it that stayed
The pillars of the universe, and formed
The amphitheatre of Heav'n?   What touch
Was that which moved the elements, and the
Azure vaults surrounded celestial worlds?
Who said, "let there be light," and merid'an
Glory passed through the trackless ether, and
Lit up those tapers through immensity
Of space?   Who rides upon the wings of the
Winds, that surround those countless worlds; and is
Worthy of all glory and pow'r throughout
His vast dominions?   Frail worm of earth! this
Is thy Father God.   What then is man?   What
His rank amid this vast machinery?
An atom of an atom world! a lost
Cypher on the left! a blank of blanks! a
Bubble on the wave.   O stop, my muse, nor
Degrade the works of God!   For in man is
Planted an immortal soul, that shall live
When those worlds shall be purified by fire!
Their heavens roll together as a scroll, and pass
Away!—a soul, that cost the blood of the
Cross to redeem it! and must sow on the
Shores of Time the seed of an eternal
Heaven or Hell.   Angels must soon be its
Companions around the throne of God, or
Dire demons lost, and Dives in the flames.
   Having with my muse far into chaos
Rode, to view those regions of primeval
Night, that brooded o'er the vast expanse! thence
Traveled down the eternal stream, to the
Period Time began, when God arose,
And with his creative mandate hung out
The starry lamps of heav'n, to diffuse their
Light to opaque orbs and satellites, like

The moon-beams on quiv'ring floods of silver!
I now return to my native earth, the
Frail mother of my existence, for a
Moment's space, in which I must make my bed
For an Immortality of Heaven's weal,
Or the woes of Hell. Here we see the lost
Pigmy tow'rs; or withers in eternal
Future, under the execration of
An angry God. What finite mind can scan
The Infinite? What pen describe his pow'r?

   As I surveyed the planetary worlds,
And viewed the wonders of creation's birth,
I, in my flight, far excelled the lightning's
Flash, or the telegraph's matchless speed. In
One moment I plucked the blooming rose; the
Next, lit on some distant star, whose swift-winged
Light has never reached our globe. O, what a
Miracle is man to man! If he so
Small, and yet so great,—how great the Author
Of his being! Yet still more wonders rise,
Towering height o'er height, and strike, with joy
Or pain, the deathless, blood-bought soul of man.
Here, O my muse, let all thy passions roll,
And tune thy harp to sing thy Descant true.

   When God had finished worlds on worlds, and flung
Them through the wilderness of space! and when
His plastic arm those countless orbs had bound
In their vast courses through the blue abyss!
Those heav'nly globes in perfect order rolled,
And felt the pow'r of their Creator's nod.
Then back he flew to the abode of man,
While yet remaining in his mother dust,
And showed the wisdom of his God-like plan,
Long made before creation took its birth.
By his Omnific wisdom, pow'r and grace,
He said, " Let us make man," and man was made:
" He in his nostrils breathed the breath of life;
And he became a living soul." Now God
Saw it was not good for man alone to

Dwell ; and he caused a deep sleep on him to
Fall; and took from his side a rib, out of
Which he woman made. So they were made, male
And female, from earth's insentient dust,
To dress the garden God for them prepared.
   All nature has laws, by her Creator
Made ; and justice demands obedience
To her great Author's name. God has showed his
Mercy in the' creation of man,—made him
Spotless as the driven snow,—perfect in
Holiness,—pure as the seraph, and a
Little lower than the angels. He gave
To him volitions of his own, with pow'r
To revere his Creator, and retain
His purity ; or obey the tempter's
Voice,—become defiled, and lose the favor
Of his God. A law was put before him,
And for the disobed'ence of which, was
The penalty of death. Soon the Serpent
Beguiled the woman, " She plucked, she ate,"—the
Woman beguiled the man,—he also took
Of the forbidden tree. Thus the holy
Twain became defiled,—incurred God's wrath, and
Were from Eden driven. In that moment
All was lost !—earth felt the wound !—groaned to her
Centre ! Heaven let fall a tear ! while Hell
Shouted in triumph through her dark domain.
O, my soul, what a fall was that ! which cursed
With two-fold death every victim slain.
   Since man has trespassed on Jehovah's laws,
And plucked the fruit his justice had forbid'n ;
Has chosen death,—excluded mercy's voice,
And sunk beneath the direful curse of Heav'n ;
God's holy light has left his fallen soul,
To range in darkness, and sadly plod its
Way in sin's forbidden path,—laden with
Guilt, sorrow, pain, and death. Ev'ry beating
Pulse tells him of his fall. Eden's glory
Exchanged for midnight gloom, shrouds his mourning

Heart, and swells his gushing tears. He is now
A poor vagrant,—his Paradise lost ! has
A frail barque,—soon to be wrecked on life's rough
Sea ! and a soul that must cast anchor on
The barren strands of Hell ! Theft, murder, and
Revenge, rankle in his bosom ! his thoughts
Are evil as the sparks ascend ! the bane
Of sin beguiles his lips ! he thirsts for blood !
And is lost to virtue, God, and Heaven.
Nor does he die alone ! His curse inspires
His progeny, and tunes their mournful harps
To swell the dirge of their temporal, and
Eternal pain. O God ! what pen shall paint
The ruins of the fall ? What scales shall weigh the'
Value of the soul, or tell the weight of
Hell's eternal doom ? What numbers count the
Wails of the lost, as they plunge the waves of
Fire, where groan follows groan, and death binds fast
To endless death ? O my God ! save from this
Gulf of despair ! this bottomless pit of woe.

   No time to idle here. Awake my muse,
And on this holy morning, thy mournful
Descant sing. E'er since the fall, the waves of
Sin in every form have rolled mountains
High,—sunk the world in wild despair,—scourged the
Rebel with wretchedness for guilt ; because God's
Wrath arose against his creature man. The
Gentle zephyrs, that bore the breezes of
Eternal life through the groves of Eden,
Have been inspired with baneful vapors ; which
Bear to suffering humanity, plagues,
Pestilence, disease and death. Ev'ry hour
Swells the groans of earth-born agonies, and
Bears to Heav'n's insulted Majesty the
History of our wrongs, and record of
Our sighs. And all this for who ? for you and
Me ;—cursed with double death. Ah, whither shall
We flee this load of wrath, which makes our frail
Spirits quake, "and turns the good man pale ?" Heav'n's

Blood shall answer, ere we close our song, when
We change the picture of this mournful tale.
　　Goodness belongs to God;—sin to men and
Devils,—groaning under chains of darkness,
God made the angels around his throne,—tuned   [white
Their golden harps,—crowned their heads,—wove their
Garments, and composed the song they sing to
His eternal honor.   He made Adam
Pure as his own Divinity ; but made
Him in the sphere of man.   Freely he stood
While he stood, and freely fell when he fell ;
So did Eve, and all Heav'n-born angels lost.
No immutable decree, passed in some
Lost date of eternity, confirmed their
Disobedience, and forced their fall. If
Not, sin belongs to God, and him alone.
Therefore we see his sentence just on men,
And angels lost, when banished from his fold.
No misery in all the worlds of God,
Ever sprung from him without a cause.   Sin
Is the cause of misery, and naught beside.
Sin drove the bolts of demons,—forged their chains,—
Shut them out of Heaven,—secured God's wrath,
And rolled the red waves of eternal fire
Through all the howling regions of the damned.
Sin drove Adam from his Eden,—barred the
Gate of Paradise,—expelled the favor
Of his God,—caused ev'ry groan of suff'ring
Humanity, and soon will wind our chains
In death, and make our last damnation sure.
Sin is a foul monster, beyond finite
Comprehension ; and none but God can solve
His pow'r, and tell the number of his slain.
　　Years rolled on, laden with wrath divine ; while
Man in folly bent, sought for bliss in earth's
Delight,—sought, but sought in vain,—run wild in
All the mazes of his soul,—by dreams and
Phantoms built his castles,—raised his Babels,—
Spurned his Lord,—slew the innocent,—sought for

Mammon,—plead for honor,—worshiped gold,—made
His gods,—a drunkard was, and showed himself
Expert in all the wilderness of sin.
Such were the crimes that called God's vengeance forth,
To scourge the world with fell disease and death.
   Now when Jehovah from his lofty throne,
Looked down upon the wickedness of man,
His eyes were pained,—his very soul grew sick,—
Repentance moved his bosom ; but not for
Himself,—for sinners lost.   Now God arose
In the vengeance of his might,—girt his sword
Upon his thigh,—his thunderbolts prepared,
And swore by his Almighty power to
Destroy the world.   The flood of his anger
Was his besom ;—he drew the sword of his
Wrath,—his thunderbolts made ready, to burst
In fearful roar, for the retribution
Of sin, and vindication of his law.
   Summer and Winter came, and passed away ·—
Years revolved in their primeval rounds ;—the
Sun smiled upon the world as in the days
Of yore ;—the moon ascended her pathway
Of stars ;—the crystal lakes rolled their clear waves
To the tune of the' piping winds ;—the oceans,
Moved by gentle gales, swelled in primitive
Grandeur ;—the rivers that swept along the
Shores of the sublime highlands, still bore their
Traffic to the briny deep ;—the stars of
Heav'n, with their gushing fires, shone on the world
In the meridian of night ; and earth
Smiled with abundant harvest, in ev'ry
Ample round.   And all this for who ? for man,—
The' vile offender,—a poor lost vagrant,—a
Robber of mercy, and rebel to God.
But suddenly the heav'ns became darkened,—·
Nature assumed a strange appearance,—the
Fountains of the great deep were broken up,—
God's flood-gates began to open, and his
Torrents fast descended on a drowning

World. The vile infidel, long warned by Noah
Of his fate, began to believe like lost
Dives ; but too late ! for Noah was shut
In, and the ark was floating on the vast
Ocean, fast rising to surround the globe.
For forty days the flood increased,—swelled the
Rivers—the rivers the oceans, until
The highest mountain was overflowed, and
All mankind, with ev'ry living substance
Found a watery grave, save Noah, and
The household of the ark. Here the skeptic,
When he had passed the bounds of mercy, felt
His guilt, and the dread sentence of his God.

Noah, and all his colleagues in the ark,
Were borne above the element of death ;
And saved to see the sun absorb the flood,
And populate this curse-doomed earth again.

The rainbow, God's bright token in the clouds,
Declares the world shall be destroyed no more,
Until the day the worthy bard has sung,
"That day for which all other days were made."

Now men increased, and as their numbers grew,
They grew in vice, and learned to sow the seed
Of death,—to vex the Lord,—increase his wrath,
And call his curse once more. Sodom, that God
Forsaken city, save by his ire, ran
Swift in every form of sin ; but soon
Felt its sting, and in oblivion wound
Its chain. Gomorrah, the twin city of
The plains, nor least in treason dyed, did rank
With foes to God,—soon lost its date among
The sons of men. For those cities, Abram
Plead ; and had there been ten righteous found
Therein, the salt had saved them from the flames.

Now God arose, and in his anger whet
His flaming sword, to drench it in the blood
Of his stern enemies ; where mercy long
Had plead, but plead in vain. Before the scourge,
He sent his angels down, to warn once more

That sin-devoted race, and sunder wide
The right'ous and the wicked.   They dwelt with
Lot 'til near the break of day, and as he
Lingered long to plead his friend's escape, they
Forced him, wife and daughters, from the city ;
And with a stern command, bade them flee for
Life ! the wife of Lot looked back,—became a
Lasting monument of sin ! while he, and
His two daughters fast fled for Zoar's hill.
Scarce had they left the cities of the plain,
Ere a storm of brimstone, surcharged with death,
Swept all their numbers to one common grave.
  Now while my muse descends the stream of Time
And of God's judgments takes a faint survey;
In rapid flight I hasten on my course,
And cast my anchor on Mount Calvary's hill.
Time is too short to mention Samson's death,
Or tell the number of Philistines slain ;
To show the folly of Goliah's threat,
When he defied the armies of the Lord.
I therefore bid those ancient scenes farewell;
Though their vast numbers meet my passing eye,
And hasten onward to Jerusalem,
When Jews by Titus with their temple fell.
  Ever since the fall, War, the foul product
Of the' monster sin, has shook the world,—destroyed
Thrones and dominions,—taken and giv'n crowns,—
Lavished silver and gold,—spread contagion,—
Poisoned disciples,—made orphans mourn,—caused
Widows' tears,—spilt rivers of blood,—destroyed
Cities and temples,—scourged the innocent,
Forged chains of slav'ry,—set free the pris'ner,—
Invaded peace,—took virtue's flag,—hardened
The heart,—poisoned the soul,—silenced the pulse,—
Destroyed good morals,—made man a demon,—
Caused the wide world to groan to its centre,
And clothed mankind in mournful weeds of woe.
War first commenced in Heaven, then took its
Abode in the breast of man ; and has proved

Itself, to be the foulest whelp of sin,
That ever invaded the worlds of God.

   Ye holy Bards,—baptized sons of Levi,—
Born of the seed of Abraham, who have
Sung the dirges of your Father's wrath and
Praise, from the days of Adam, to the date
Of Jerusalem's fallen grandeur; draw
Near with your solemn songs of weal and woe,—
Compose my Descant, and aid me to strike
The mournful music of Salem's final groan.
This frightful theme makes my sad heart to bleed,—
My soul to quake,—and drowns my eyes in tears.
O, that my pen were able for this task!
To paint in full the Jew's untimely doom.

   To the Jews God gave his holy law,—made
His covenant,—inspired them with light,—called
Them his people,—blessed them with his favor,
And gave to them all the rich graces of
The sons of God; while the poor Gentile, was
Left to wander in the labyrinth of
Vice, and error,—a stranger to virtue,
Reason, hope, and Heav'n. But God's mercies were
Slighted:—the Jews were often scourged for guilt;
But sinned again. These are they that killed the
Servants of the living God, and at last
Slew the Savior in their curse-doomed city.
In the superstition, and blindness of
Their hearts, they incurred Jehovah's wrath, to
Fall on them according to the presage
Of his Son, until their streets were crimsoned
With their own blood, and not one stone in all
Their walls and tow'rs was left upon another.
The temple's veil was rent,—its key-stone was
Broke, and ere that generation passed, by
The forbidden fire-brand of the Roman
Soldier, it fell beneath its burning flames.

   Ere the destruction of the Jews the bright
Harbingers of God left the celestial
City, and with signs and wonders foretold

Their doom.   For the space of six months a drawn
Sword hung over Jerusalem ! martial
Chariots with their charioteers, and
Horsemen with trumpets, were seen in the heav'ns,
Maneuvering as on the battle field !
The pond'rous gates of the city walls were
Found unbarred by angels ! an heifer in
The temple for sacrifice, brought forth a
Lamb ! a prophetic Jew, stood on the walls
Day and night, and cried, " woe be unto this
City !" and last of all, " woe be unto
Myself also !" and he fell by the dart
Of his enemy.   But this is not all,
A Savior, after he had wept over
Jerusalem, plead for their salvation
With his groans and tears, and after all he
Could do, being unable to move their
Hearts, he exclaimed, " behold your house is left
Unto you des'late ! and ye shall not see
Me henceforth, 'till ye shall say blessed is
He that cometh in the name of the Lord."
In spite of all these warnings, the lost Jews
Bent on evil, and veiled in unbelief,
Remained strangers to salvation, until
The flames of their Jerusalem portrayed
Their certain doom, and forged their pond'rous chains
At last they cried to God for help! but in
Their prayer there was no cry, " Jesus save."
  The Jew in his own esteem, could like the
Giant condor, ascend the heavens above
Mortal sight, and leave the poor Gentile in
Regions far below.   But soon the Heathen
Took the flight of the eagle, and left the
Lost Jew to feel his curse-bowed grandeur, and
Smoulder beneath the ruin of his flames.
  Now the Jews believed Jehovah, as in
The days of yore, would still their city save.
Though there had been signs in heaven, and the
Predictions and warnings of God's only

Son, to confirm their overthrow ; yet they
Feared no evil.   As the dreamless sleeper
Lays down in quietude, fearless of his
Danger near ; so with the Jews, blinded in
Their zeal, until Titus them did beseige.
    The dread conflict now begins ! the Jews are
Shut in ! the ponderous engine beats their
Walls ! the columns remain firm at their posts !
The Jews full of confusion have lost their
Strength ! starvation weakens their ranks ! and
Threatens greater slaughter than their foes ! while
Titus, steady to his trust, is forcing
His way through the walls ! he enters, and now
Begins the scene of death.   The trumpet sounds
The charge ! the colors are flying ! and the
Roman eagle is waving over the
Ranks of the enemy.   Now is one wild
Scene of battle ! the poniard, sabre, and
Spear, spill the blood of the Jews.   Some fall on
Their own swords ! others cast lots to see who
Will slay their number, rather than be slain
By their foes ! while through the streets the crimson
Stream of life's rich torrent flows.   A strange light,
In the merid'an of day, begins to
Ascend the heavens !   Jerusalem is
On fire !—the temple flames in terrific
Grandeur ! while every surviving Jew
Begins to tremble through all the' Holy Land.
'Tis done ! the scene is over !—the city
Of God in ruins ! and her des'lation
Alone has destroyed the hope of the Jew.
    All the power, glory, and affluence,
Of which the Jew could boast, have passed away,
And left him forsaken of his God,—in
Wild despair.   The land of Judea is
Now without temple or altar ! and the
Wandering Jew, branded and scorned for guilt,
Yet remains the enemy of Jesus !—
His only Redeemer, and only God.

On the plains of Syria, and the Mount
Of Calvary, the homaged birth-place of
The world's Redemption, instead of the flag
Of the Cross, the Saracen banner spreads
Its sable folds, and their minarets and
Bastions ascribe to Mahomet's glory,—
The vile impostor, and the Pagan's god.
The warrior, that vindicates his prophet's
Heav'n, treads careless on the sacred dust of
Departed saints, as if the Lamb of God
Had never preached his free salvation there.
    Having briefly touched upon the scenes of yore,
When God poured forth his ire on aliens lost ;
I hasten onward down the stream of Time,
To sing of Corsica's triumphant son ;
Who with his martial glory fired the world
And made all Europe tremble at his nod.
Frenchmen, I speak of your departed king,
Whose high ambition raised him to his throne ,
But pressing pow'r beyond its worthy bounds,
Destroyed his sceptre, and his glory fell.
British and Prussian sons, combined to clip
His wings,—forge his chains, and dispossess him
Of his martial reign.   The tyrant fell at
The siege of Waterloo, amid the roar
Of cannon, booming on the midnight air.
    Bonaparte was the monster of his age !
He lit up the world with the flames of war !
Conquered kingdoms,--destroyed thrones,--extinguished
Crowns,—razed monasteries,—enfranchised nuns,—
Made the Pope tremble,—set his prisoners
Free,—diffused moral poison,—made widows
And orphans,—involved kingdoms,—spilt rivers
Of blood,—lavished mammon,—burnt cities,—made
Deists and infidels,—scourged the world,—drove his
Char'ot over groans and death,—sailed on seas
Of blood,—trained his soldiers for a two-fold
Hell,—slew the innocent, and strode like a
Demon over the empires of Europe.

And all for what ? for that desire of fame,
Which forged his chains on St. Helena's isle.

  We now trace this murderer in his course
Through the Russian campaign ! We begin at
The siege of Smolensko, where a hundred
Cannon from the stern ranks of the Russians
Poured upon the French columns with dreadfu'
Slaughter ! while in return they sent back a
More terrible carnage ! The battle raged in
Desperate fury ! but in spite of the
Russian force, the enemy passed over
The entrenched suburbs, and fought at the point
Of the bay'net ! The earth was strewn with the
Dead and dying !—blood in torrents ran !—the
Shrieks of the wounded rent the air, while the
Russians returned to Smolensko, to meet
A more terrible doom ! The French pursued
Them to the city, and recommenced the
Work of death ! Vast numbers in both armies
Fell, ere Napol'on's standard triumphed in
The cap'tal, mid the ruins of the flames.

  We now approach the scene of Borodino,
On that mem'rable day, when thousands for
The last time beheld the light ! The moment
Had arrived, when the awful discharge of
Two thousand cannon, was to break the deep
Silence of expectation, and arouse
In those mighty armies all the terrors
Of war ! The charge of the French columns on
Bagrations ranks, made a horrible slaughter !
Yet Napol'on pressed the battle to his
Lines, over the bastions of the dead, which
Had fallen to rise no more ! The conflict
Raged with terrible carnage, while thousands
Of cannon answered cannon, the smoke of
Which shut out the sun from the field of death !
The sabres of forty thousand dragoons
Clashed in horrid gloom, while countless bay'nets,
Bursting through the sable vapor, strowed the

Pattle field with blood, and mountains of the slain.
The approaching night closed the scene of that
Sanguinary day, which swept to the grave
Near eighty thousand soldiers from the field.
   Napol'on's thirst for blood and fame increased!
He looked forward to the treasures, towers,
And min'rets of Moscow, with an eagle's
Eye, and pulse high bounding for victory,—
Expecting a refuge from the scourging
Element! On September fourteenth, his
Army appeared before the city!—his
Guards entered the gate in hope of conquest!—
His troops moved for the Kremlin!—the Russians
Had taken refuge there,—closed their gates, and
Struggled for defence!—The French found their way
     through,—
Sacrificed their innocent victims, and
Soon spread over the city, committing
Ravages beyond expression! The streets,
Houses, and cellars flowed with blood!—manhood
Was lost in the French soldier!—he was like
The lion in search of prey!—was dyed with
Every crime! for Napoleon had
Promised his troops the treasures of Moscow.
   To destroy the asylum of the French
Army, the Russians fired their city! The
Soldiers enraged at the sight, increased their
Outrage and slaughter like fiends incarnate!
The flames enraged!—the Kremlin took fire! and
The glory of Moscow sunk in ruins.
   Bonaparte, with disappointed hope, left
The city, to meet the scourge of freezing
Elements,—the swift descending snows, and
Approaching frosts of Winter; which threatened
Death and despair to his army; while the
Russians pursued him in his retreat with
A horrible slaughter. The dogs with their
Frightful howl, and clouds of ravens hov'ring
Over the dead, presaged their doom, and struck

The boldest hearts with terror.   Their supposed
Refuge at Smolensko had been destroyed,—
All their provisions consumed,—the ninth corps
Had gone, and those soldiers without shelter
That encamped in the street, were found dead at
The fires they had kindled.   For the space of
Three leagues from this point, the road was strown with
The dead and dying around the green boughs
They had sought to inflame.   Already since
The retreat, Napol'on had lost by the
Russians, fatigue, and famine, near eighty
Thousand men.   And for what? to satiate
The vain ambition of his mad career.

 We now approach the' scene of Beresina,
The climax of the campaign, in which were
The' vilest acts of sin, and deepest stains of
Human guilt.   Close pursued by the Russians the'
French were in haste to cross the bridge ;—a strife
Rose between the foot soldiers, and dragoons,
To see which should first secure their passage,
And thousands were slain in this sore conflict ;
Which formed a mountain of the dead at the
Mouth of the bridge, that were crushed by horses,
And wheels of artillery.   At length the
Enemy hove in sight, and the struggle
Beggared description.   Thousands despaired of
All hope, plunged into the Beresina
To die.   Having passed over, they burnt the
Bridge, and left in the hands of the Russians
More than twenty thousand of the sick and
Wounded.   The enemy approached their prey !--
The night w: s dark and wild! but a darker
Night veiled the hearts of those dying soldiers.

 We still pass on and behold Napol'on
Struck with fear and guilt, made his desertion.
His soldiers cried, " is he who lavished our
Blood afraid to die with us ?"   Expiring
Warriors still continued to fall, and their   ·
Flesh was often eaten by their starving

Comrades. Some sat down on lifeless bodies
Around the fire they had kindled, and when
It was extinguished, being unable
To rise, they fell by the side of the dead.
Others plunged themselves into the flames, and
Died in horrid convulsions. When a worn
Out soldier fell, the next would rob him of
All he possessed. His cry was, " O help! they
Rob me! they murder me !" but they heard not
His prayer. Naked amid the freezing
Elements, wild beasts, and vultures of prey
They left him in all the horrors of war,
To weep and die in deep-toned agonies.
O my God! are these the savage acts of
Thy creatures, amid the Gospel of light,
And the regen'rating blood of the Cross ?
  I might mention the battle of Waterloo,
The last conflict of Napol'on ! I might
Tell of the twenty thousand, that strowed the
Field of the slain, on that mem'rable day !
I might show Bonaparte's fierce ambition,
As he poured fresh columns on the English
Lines, when Wellington wiped the sweat from his
Face, and prayed that Blucher, or night would come.
I might tell of the dire curse shown on his
Brow, and the fearful emotions of his
Heart, when he saw the Prussians bursting the
Distant wood ! I might display his spirit's
Wrath, when he sent his imper'al guard, to
Pour fresh slaughter on the British columns !
I might tell of Napoleon's last hope,
When the Prussians gave the second discharge
Of artillery on the enemy,
As they wheeled and flew ! The battle is lost !
And Wellington has taken the field ! The French
Tyrant fled, pursued by the cannons' roar.
  Bonaparte is bound to rage no more ! Like
The wild tiger caged, he may thirst for blood,
But he shall thirst in vain ! As the king of
21

Birds, he could soar the heavens of his martial
Glory, and behold the storm, and lightnings
Play below ; but he shall not soar again !
The distant island of the sea has caged
Him, and he has become a doomed pris'ner !
His soldiers that have survived their dangers,
Shall no longer fear his voice, or tremble
At his nod !   Never again shall he breathe
The pure air of freedom, or terrify
The world with his sanguine revolutions ;
For his stronger foes have chain'd him, and in
His fetters he shall die.   Amid the wild
Tempest, and the waves lashing themselves far
Upon the island, the last stages of
A corroding cancer drink his blood, while
His spirit in its expiring struggle
Is watching the current of battle.   His
Sun is about to set in darkness, mid
Fountains of tears,—streams of blood, and oceans
Of woe ;—caused by the ambition of this
Expiring conqueror.   The nations shall breathe free ;—
For his sun has gone down to rise no more.
    The man that sheds the blood of his fellow
For envy,—ambition, or gold, is a
Murderer,—the brother of Cain,—the vile
Slave of the devil ; and will so be judged
At the last great day.   The reason why the
Gospel is so dormant in flooding the
World with its light, is because Pagans look
On Europe and America, and say,
" How these Christians murder one another ?"
There is no evil this side the regions
Of eternal despair, that compares to
War.   It is the fruit of demons, and their
Colleagues incarnate.   On this theme I say
No more ; but drop my pen, and sigh farewell.
    Having sung of the besoms of God's wrath,
And of war, man's vilest instrument for
The untimely destruction of a world ;

I now hasten to the angel of death,
That drives the chariot of the ire of
God over the vast millions of his slain.
    My muse once more awake, still strike thy harp
In tones of woe, that rend the heart, and scourge
The world.   My Descant now is death,—written
On the flag, borne by the pale horse and his
Rider, in sable capitals.   He makes
All flesh to kiss the dust from whence it rose.
His vast dominion is the known empire
Of a fallen world;—his commission is
From Him who gave the sentence, and his pow'r
Shall never cease 'till all mankind are slain.
He has no mercy ;—to him pardon is
A lost stranger, since justice wove his crown.
This stern king has waved his banner over
All flesh ever since the fall of Adam ;
And will ride forth in victory, until
The trumpet of the first resurrection.
    Ye sad victims of this conqueror, can
You tell me what it is to die, and pass
The River of Jordan ?   Can you unfold
To me the frightful sensations, when the
Clay building begins to sink beneath the
Throes of convulsive agony, and the
Chills of death to freeze every flowing
Vein ?   Can you explain to me the deep woes
Of the mind as the' heart begins to faint, and
The gangrene to destroy the extremities
Of life ?   Can you show me the internal
Strife of soul and body, indicated
By the ghastly visage writhing in the
Groans of dissolution ?   Can you tell of
The solemn farewell of the departing
Spirit, as she sits on the quiv'ring lips
Of mortality, ready to close her
Accounts with earth, and take her flight to God ?
I pause for a reply ; but receive no
Answer.   The beholder may sympathize his

Dying friend, and be moved to tears ; but to
Him this is not death.   No finite mind can
Convey to the human understanding
The vast weight of expiring agonies.

Death has no respect of persons, but makes
Universal triumph o'er his victims.
The black and white, rich and poor, young and old,
King and beggar, are all destroyed by the
Same tyrant.   The youth, in the fashions and
Amusements of life, glorying in the
Theatre, or dark dens of pollution,
Must fall a prey to the same conqueror.
The man in life's meridian, seeking
The vain riches and honors of the world,
Or rejoicing in its vanities, shall
Drink the sad cup of death.   The king on his
Throne, who extends his arm of pow'r, must fall
By the sword of this grim monster.   The slave,
In chains of bondage, shall feel his sanguine
Streams of life expiring, and sleep on the
Same dreamless bed, as that of his master.

Ye frail sons of earth, robed in glory, or
Wading the depths of penury and pain,
Come reason with death !—meditate the hour
When you must bow down under your last strong
Agony,—the world recede from your sight,—
Your friends take their long farewell,—your eyes close
For the last time,—the wheels of life stand still,
And your barques founder in the dreamless tomb.
Forestall your fate !—for there is no escape !—
The shroud,—the coffin,—the funeral pall,—
The narrow house, and gnawing worm are yours.
Look upon the sun, moon and stars with their
Gushing fires ;—behold the lake,—the island,—
The river, and mountain, and remember
That ere long you shall see them not again.
Your earth or ocean graves, that have received
You with many tears, shall your images
Deface, and the mould that has nourished your

Growth, to return to prior dust, will soon
Transform you to the sundry elements
Of nature, to be brothers of briny
Waves,—flinty rocks,—mountain oaks,—the food of
Man, or the isentient clod, turned by
The planter's slave, or ploughshare of the swain.
   But in your last slumber you shall not rest
Alone. You shall lay down with the ancient
Patriarchs,—with kings that swayed their golden
Sceptres,—the stars of earth,—the wise and good,
And the holy seers of gone by ages.
The lakes and oceans with their rolling waves,—
The murmuring brooks that flow the verdant
Meads,—the swelling rivers that sweep along
The sublime highlands,—the vales extended
Between the lofty hills, and the mountains
Iron-bound,—ancient as creation's birth, all
Conspire to adorn the vast tomb of man.
The sun and moon, and all the lamps of heav'n,
Have shone on earth's common grave since Adam
Died. The legions, that now tread this wide earth,
Are few to those that sleep in its bosom.
Let your souls take wing, and the African
Desert pierce ;—view Iceland's eternal frosts !
Then light on the Rocky Mountains, where the
Missouri hears no murmur but its own !
Yet in those dark regions, millions since Time
Began, have laid them down in their last sleep.
   So shall you rest amid earth's revolving
Ages, while the thoughtless ones will cease to
Think of your departure : but there is no
Loss in that ; for weeping cannot raise the
Dead, or save the living from the tomb. All
That breathe must share your fate. The careless, in
Folly bent, will laugh o'er your dust, and sport
In the phantoms of their brain ;—the vain pomp
Of earth shall swell their songs, and drive from them
The solemn thoughts of death ; yet all these gay
And simple ones shall forget their wine and

Mirth, and make their bed with you.   As the length
Of Time revolves away, the race of men,—
Son and sire,—maid and matron,—prince and slave,—
The fair infant and giant form, shall be
Borne along to join the departed dead,
And swell the bosom of earth's common grave.
   The pains of death are greatly enhanced, or
Mitigated, according to the prospect
Of a future state.   Some have died in the
Full expectation of Heaven, others
Under the most frightful prospects of Hell.
Such was the case of dying Altamont.
His disease indicated approaching
Dissolution ; but more terrible was
The disease of his mind.   His unkindness
Had murdered his wife ; his dissipation
Beggared his boy ; and his sins destroyed his
Soul.   His confession was, " I have neither
Life nor hope.   I have spurned my God,—denied
His Son, and plucked his ruin.   Oh Time !   Time '
Thou art lost ! forever lost in the swift
Madness of my soul.   Oh for a month ! a
Week, to wash away my sins !   But I plead
In vain.   Time has wove my winding sheet, and
Made my grave in Hell.   To me all Heaven
Is lost.   Already I begin to feel
The gnawings of the worm that never dies.
This soul is full mighty to reason, full
Powerful to suffer ! and must soon survive
The pangs of death, and prove itself immortal.
And as for God, nothing less could cause the
Pains I feel.   Didst thou endure the mountain
Of guilt upon me, thou wouldst struggle with
The martyr for his stake, and bless Heav'n for
Those flames that are not an eternal fire.
My principles have poisoned the world !   And
Is there yet another Hell ?   Oh ! thou most
Indulgent God !   Hell is a refuge, if
It hide me from thy frown."   Soon after his

Reason failed ;—his frightful appearance told
Of horrors not to be repeated, or
Ever forgotten!   And ere the sun had
Gilded the eastern horizon, this gay,
Noble, and most wretched Altamont died.
   We now invert the picture, and portray
Another personage, that fell in the
Days of her youth by fatal consumption.
Her form was the symmetry of beauty ;—
She was the object of her parent's love ;—
And the fair rose of the morning glories.
Health smiled upon her cheek, and long life was
Her prospect.   But suddenly her fond hopes
Were blasted ;—the' destroyer came, and in his
Assault, chained his victim with the disease
Of death.   Aid was called for, but in vain was
The arm of man ; for her case was mortal,
And knew of no reprieve.   But thank God, she
Was not like the dying queen, that cried, "a
Million of money for a moment of
Time"! but stood firm on the Rock of Ages.
Her parents had taught her Jesus, and she
Found her Savior.   She felt her sins all washed
Away in the blood of atonement, and
Like Paul she was ready to die.   Truly
Through the Jordan of death, was a dreary
Passport ; but when she saw her Savior had
Perfumed the grave for the believer, and
Planted the flow'rs of Heav'n's eternal spring
In the moss of the dark sepulchre, her
Soul shouted for joy, and triumphed o'er her
Last en'my.   Death steady to his purpose,
Pursued her close through ev'ry lane of life !
At length she felt the fatal moment near,
When, like a bird freed from his cage, she should
Burst her clay prison, and go home to God.
She called her parents around her dying
Bed,—thanked them for those lessons that preached the
Savior,—admonished them to adorn their

Profession by a holy life,—then bade
Them her last farewell.   And after making
A solemn preparation by pray'r, uttered
The last groan of mortality, and the
Swift winged angels bore her home to God.

   Having worn out my harp on the sad dirge
Of a dying world, and much exhausted
The harper's strength, I will attempt to string
It anew for a brighter theme, and by
The grace of God, give the pleasing tune of
The world's Redemption by the' blood of the Cross.

   The bound prisoner, sentenced to his dark
Cell without hope of future exemption,
Is an object of extreme despair.   But
Mercy revives his hope,—his reprieve is
Granted,—is borne to his ear,—he shouts for
Joy,—leaps like the bounding roe in the fresh
Breezes of heav'n, and imparts his gracious
Thanks to his liberal benefactor.

   But how faint the emblem?   I see the lost
Sinner in his mire and pollution, with
His sentence from the lips of the' Eternal,
Which bound him in the first and second death
Thus without God, he was lost in the gloom
Of night, where no ray of light could beam on
His pathway,—no created arm burst his chains.
There dwelt the mournful prisoner alone,
Doomed by that law which knew of no reprieve.

   But a God began to move in mercy
For an apostate world.   A voice was heard
Through Heav'n, "lo I come"!   At this the harps of
Angels were mute, and they stood amazed, that
God the Son should cast off his crown.   Amid
The throng of seraphim and cherubim,
He laid by the raiment of his glory,—
Bade farewell to Heaven's shining millions,
And with the flight of a God descended
From his throne,—made the manger his cradle,
And his birth place the' stable of Bethlehem.

By this condescension,—his subsequent
Sufferings on the Cross, and his triumph
Over the grave,—he trod upon the world's
Last en'my, and fastened to his char'ot
Wheels the conquered millions of death and Hell!
   To describe the Savior's sufferings for
Man's redemption, my soul takes wing to the
Garden of Gethsemane, and beholds
His agony as he fell on his face
And prayed to God. There the blessed Jesus,
With blood pressing through ev'ry pore, bore the
Pond'rous load of human guilt, which would have
Crushed a world to Hell. In his midnight woes,
With his soul sorrowful even unto
Death, and his human'ty sinking under
The load of guilt he bore, an angel drew
Near, and strengthened the suff'ring Son of God.
   We now hasten to Calvary's horrid
Eminence,—to the Savior's dying hour.
He was condemned by his own creation,
And spiked to the cursed wood. They reared him
Up, a spectacle to Heaven and earth,
Amid the sneers of the Jew and Gentile
Throng. His temples were mangled with a crown
Of thorns,—his hands and feet cleft with rugged
Irons,—his body covered with wounds, and his
Soul pierced with extreme agonies. At this
Phenomenon, nature could no longer
Endure the suff'rings of her Creator
She vibrated with horror through all her
Dominions. The sun shrouded in darkness,
Rolled back his char'ot, and refused to
Shine for the space of three hours, on the curs'd
Abode of man. The mountains quaked,—the rocks
Rent,—the earth trembled, and the temple's veil
Was rent in twain. Lost angels heard the cry
Of the world's redemption, and they howled through
All their dark domains, while death let fall the
Chains that bound his pris'ners, and they started

22

Into life.   Jesus knowing that all things
Were accomplished, he cried with a loud voice,
" It is finished, and he gave up the Ghost."
    Glory to God! that redemption by the
Cross was not confined to Jews, or a part
Of the Gentiles; but was made for "the sins
Of the whole world."   That when Jesus cried, " It
Is finished, and bowed his head and died," he
Then made an atonement for all mankind.
Here we see the Savior's sacrifice has
Made it possible for ev'ry slave, to
Burst his chains through faith in redeeming blood,
And escape the woes of the second death.
    Ye potentates, that wield your vast sceptres
Over empires, and fare sumptuously
Ev'ry day, come lay your honor at the
Feet of this King, who spilt his blood for your
Souls' redemption.   Ye nobles of the earth,
Whose chariots bear you above the wants
Of penury, come drink the healing streams,
And feast on the rich banquet of Calv ry.
Ye vile murd'rers, that drove the spear into
Your Savior's side, repent of your deepest
Stains of guilt, and through faith receive pardon
In his blood.   Ye lost vagrants, bowed by the
Scourge of poverty, having neither home
Nor friends, come find a refuge in your Lord.
Ye disappointed ones, whose hearts have been
Wounded by the blasted flowers of Time,
Pluck the fair rose of Sharon, and your lost
Hopes shall wound no more.   Ye that seek for the
Falling crowns of earth, forego your doubtful
Toil, and take the rich garland purchased by
The sad Victim of the cross.   Let ev'ry
Lost one forsake his way, and believe in
The sacrificial death of the Son of
God, and he shall be found of him in the
Great day of God Almighty and the Lamb.
    When the Savior had given up his life

Upon the cross, and entered the dreary
Sepulchre, his disciples believed his
Tomb to be the grave of Immortality.
But soon reviving hope inspired their hearts,
When the guard were palsied by the pow'r of
God,—the stone rolled back from the door,—the grave
Opened,—the body of Jesus not there,
And a well known voice said, "Mary"! then his
Loved ones rejoiced in hope, to see their Lord;
And they embraced their triumphant Savior.
   Cæsar's seal, and Pilate's men of war, could
No longer bind the Prisoner. Death gave
Up his chains into the hands of Him by
Whom death itself shall die. As a man he
Humbled himself to enter the grave; but
As a God he burst the tomb in vict'ry,—
Took the keys of death and hell, and placed them
In his wounded side,—rose immortal,—was
Death's last plague, and the grave's exulting King.
   Nor has Jesus risen alone. By his
Exultation he has secured the last
Triumph of ev'ry saint from his bed of
Dust! "For if Christ be risen, then shall we
Also be raised." There will be a period
In the history of Time, when the sun
Shall be darkened,—the moon turned to blood, and
The stars fall from heaven like leaves of Autumn.
Then shall the trump of the archangel sound,
And the right'ous dead shall burst their marble
Shrines, to die no more. Nor they alone! For
The last trump is yet to sound, at the voice
Of which, the wide earth must tremble to her
Centre,—the oceans swell with tremendous
Commotion,—the elements melt with fervent
Heat,—the heav'ns roll together as a scroll,
And the flames of conflagration destroy
This heinous abode of man. Then shall earth's
Cemetery give up the millions of
Its wicked dead,—never to sleep again.

O my God! into what terror would it
Strike our frightful souls, should thy dread lightnings
Now begin to thwart these heavens above,
And thy rending thunders to shake the world!
    But I hear a voice from unbelief, " the
Dead shall never rise." Infidel wisdom
Denies the pow'r of God to raise the dust
Of man,—combined with sundry elements.
The skeptic, bound fast to nature's laws, is
Forgetful of her Creator's power,—
Expels the act of miracle from his
Faith,—limits Jehovah's might, and rides in
His car of oblivion to future life.
But we are not of those that close the door
Of Heav'n,—deny God's omnipotence, and
In eternal annihilation sleep.
That voice which said, "let there be light,—let the
Worlds revolve,—let stars bedeck the heavens,—
Let Adam live," and in type of what shall
Be, said " Lazarus come forth," shall awake
Our dust from the sleep of ages to a
Life of Immortality. Nor shall we
Live alone! The Savage wild,—the polished
Greek,—the Tongousian ranger,—the dwarf
Icelander,—the Amazonian, and
Scottish chief, that for gone by ages have
Sunk in death's embrace, and through the changes
Of Time, exist in the curly vapors,—
The blades of grass,—ocean's waves, or earthly
Clods, shall hear the resurrection trumpet,
And live to die no more. Nor they alone!
All the race of Adam that have died, or
Will, before the trump shall sound, shall hear the
New creating fiat, shake off their chains
And rise in triumph o'er their vanquished king.
    My Descant now approaches the final
Day of retribution for a risen,
And congregated world. The vast millions
Since the days of Adam, have already

Heard the angel's trumpet, and burst the bonds
Of their dreamless sepulchres.   They now wait
For that voice which calls to judgment.   The judge
Assumes the glory of his pow'r,—he sits
On his brilliant throne,—is surrounded by
Clouds of angels,—is clothed with flaming fire —
His eyes sparkling with light exceeding the
Blazing meteor,—his head encircled
With brilliancy surpassing the mid-day
Sun,—his feet like unto fine brass, holding
In his hands the seven stars,—he wears a
Royal diadem,—he appears!   "But how
Unlike the man that died on Calvary."
His mandate now assembles the countless
Millions around his majestic glory;—
Waiting in awful suspense to hear their
Final doom.   This is the day for which man
Was made,—for which the sun has shone,—for which
Time has been, and for which Heav'n's blood stained the
Soldier's driven spear.   The great day of dread
Decision, that drives the unshaken bolts
Of Hell's dark domain, which bind the sinner
With lost demons in the red waves of fire!
And crowns the saint with the blood-bought garland
Of the Cross,—the fadeless robe of Heav'n,—the
Golden harp, and song of eternal life.
This the day of God Almighty's wrath, and
Of the Lamb.   At thought of this, each mundane
Wish lets go its eager grasp, and catches
At the faintest hope of Heav'n.   The earth had
Never seen a larger host than when the
Foe of Greece spread o'er the land; but this was
Small compared to the army of the skies.
Mid this clould of witnesses, the redeemed of
The Lord will lift up their heads rejoicing;
While the wicked, stung with keen remorse, shall
Linger in wild despair to meet their doom.
   The raging warrior, whose glory has been
For vict'ry and honor,—who steeled his heart

Against the prayer of his victim,—assumed
The right of God to scourge the world without
His mandate,—drove his chariot over
Thousands of his slain,—showed himself a fiend
Incarnate, is now caught in the judgment
Sentence, to inherit the dark world of woe!

   The foul murd'rer! the vilest object of a
Fallen world! who for the love of gold, and
The want of humanity, has taken
The life of the innocent! and what proves
His guilt of the blackest dye, he has laid
In ambush, and buried himself in guile
To shed blood.   But an Almighty arm has
Bound him, " hand and foot!" and the deputized
Angel of the Judge casts him into fire,
Where red waves of sorrow shall follow wave!

   The poor drunkard, that wallows in the mire,—
Makes a beast of what God made man,—poisons
Soci'ty,—degrades his wife and children,—
Wastes his scanty living,—disturbs the peace,—
Destroys his health,—blasts his mind, and becomes
A nuisance to God and man, is found at
The judgment far on the left, while the voice
Of Jesus proclaims his verdict, " depart,"
And he plunges the flames of " wrath to come !'

   The alcoholic vender, that spreads the
Bane of death among the masses,—for love
Of gold makes inebriates,—beggars their
Helpless offspring,—inverts peace to war,—weaves
The pall of despair,—digs untimely graves,—
Shortens the day of grace,—blasts the parent's
Hope,—makes youth and age insane, and tremens
With forestalling woe, to shake its victims
Over the yawning gulf!—now stands aghast,
To wail his doom in " everlasting fire!"

   The vile Deist that spurned the sinner's Hope,—
The world's Redeemer,—the Rock of defence,—
The Oblation for guilt, and the only
Star that ever shone on a fallen world,

Void of prelibation has appeared at
This final scene. What phenomenon meets
His sight! He beholds a Man he never
Knew but to spurn,—the despised Nazarene
That prayed in Gethsemane. But justice
Has caught him, and his retribution is
At hand. The dark veil of unbelief has
Fled ;—death has failed to be eternal sleep ;—
The son of Mary is now the Son of
God ;—immortal weal or woe belongs to
Man ;—miracles were by Messiah wrought ;—
He raised a Lazarus from the grave ;—the
Widow's son,—healed diseases,—stilled the waves,—
Cast out devils, and arose triumphant
O'er his tomb. All this he now believes,—but
Too late ! for his faith makes lost angels quail,
And sinners mourn that died in unbelief.
The Judge displays his wrath,—his lightnings gleam,
His thunders roar, and his expedition
Binds fast the skeptic in " the second death."
For he that spurns the Son, dispels a crown,
And plucks a thorn his withered soul to sting.
 The vain Atheist, raised from the grave of
Centuries amid the burning fires of
The resurrection morn, stands aghast at
This mournful scene, and wails the sentence of
His final doom. A God he doubts no more,—
His unbelief is gone,—his faith is now
Complete; but such as devils feel in chains
Of woe. No more he spurns the notice of
The sun,—the gushing stars,—the silver moon,—
The satelites opaque, and nature's book
As proof of God. No more his voice shall swell
With serpent hiss, and foul revenge, to mar
The great Supreme, and list disciples to
Weave their pall for death. Never again will
He God's book a fiction call,—his Lord an
Imposter vile, with obdurate heart and
Eyes excluding light. Poor man ! with frantic

Shrick he sinks beneath Jehovah's ire, and
Waits in dread despair to take the shroud, that
Veils the spirit for the tomb.   Hark ! I hear
His sentence !   " Go," saith the Judge, " bind him
Hand and foot," to share the fate of demons lost.
Too late he pleads ! for mercy's day is past,—
His verdict given, and his spirit damned.
Such is the fate of those, who wisdom drive
From sight, when in God's holy balance weighed.
    I see another cloud of ghastly fiends,
Gathered from the grave of ages, wailing
Mid this countless throng.   They stand before the
Avenger of blood ! the Man they reviled,—
Buffeted,—spit upon,—scourged,—mocked, and
        crowned,
With a thorny wreath.   But how changed !   He is
No more the incarnate son of Mary,
Arraigned before Pilate's bar !   No more he
Intercedes for the Jews that clamored for
His blood !   No more he pleads for his murd'rers
Mid the groans of his crucifixion !   No
More with tears he endures the burlesque of
Sinners ! but claims the glory he possessed
Ere the world began.   The Jews no longer
Spurn their King ; but own his scepter as lost
Spirits own.   He now assumes his pow'r,—calls
His angels forth, and with a dread command
That makes the guilty soul shed tears of blood,
He drives them out, where "utter darkness" weaves
Their pall,—where tears fall on tears,—sighs follow
Sighs,—groans toll of groans, and sorrow treads on
Eternal sorrows.   No longer justice
Waits for these, who cried a Barabbas free,
To crucify the only Son of God.
    The worldling vain, for terrene glory bound ;—
Aspired his gods in all their sundry forms ;—
Drank from the wells of earth's polluted fount
In filthy draughts that never quenched his
Thirst :—but still he cried for more.   Perchance in

Madness he arose the hill, the miser
Scaled ; and with nerves of steel, and iron grasp,
His char'ot drove o'er suff'ring poor, with ears
Closed,—a marble heart, and eyes that never
Wept for woe.   Perchance he run to gain a
Crown of some terrestrial birth in honor's
Field; and by his treach'rous course he soared to
Cabinets of fame, or presidential
Seat, with heart unconscious of his country's
Weal, as if no higher courts his deeds in
Requisition called.   He may be one that
Reveled in the midnight hour at the viol's
Alluring chant,—the gambler's sad resort,—
Pollution's foulest den,—the drunkard's vile
Retreat, or the vain fashions of a lost
World's delight, in all its blandish forms.   Such
Are the gods that blind the worldling's heart, till
Mercy's eyes have ceased to weep, and judgment
Fires send forth their flames to blast his dying soul.
He mourns ! but too late !— Heav'n's gate is closed!
        the
Books appear!—his doom is sealed!—his sentence
Giv'n!—which digs his grave mid lost angels' tombs,
    The sanguine king, that gloried in his shame,
With trembling nerve, and craven heart now meets
His Judge! that Judge who lives to die no more.
Death took his fading crown mid revolving
Empires,—streams of blood,—the saint's expiring
Groan,—the'pris'ner's galling chain,—his hostile reign
O'er subjects of his charge;—and when, Nero
Like, he drove his martial steeds through widows'
Tears,—the Christian slew,—spurned the King of kings;
Then with a foundered barque, and hellish groan,
He cast his anchor in a demon's grave.
But by the trump his vault was shook ;—his ear
Deaf was called to hear; and his mortal dust
Immortal made, now meets the Monarch of
The skies.   Amazed he stands with scepter lost,
Mid earth's vain kings that held their dying crowns.

But how sad the scene!   No more he shuns his
Retribution just!—no more evades the
Sentence of his Judge! for the great day of
His wrath has come! in which the' monarch, stained
    with
Blood, shall die to kill no more.   This is he,
Who slew the saints in God's redeeming light ;—
Drew his sword against Messiah's claims ;—saved
The guilty in forbidden sins; and braved
The terrors of the judgment day.   As the
Fool he died amid the Gospel's sound,—the
Pure blood of the Cross, and Jesus' triumph
O'er the tomb.   Such is the fate of him, who
For terrene scepters of mortal pinions
Born, sold a crown lost "worlds want wealth to buy. '
   Another monster born in human shape,
Bearing the stamp of hypocrite by name,
In lone despair now meets the judgment fires,
And wails the sentence of his final doom.
This is he, who on the shores of Time for
Love of gold, assumed the right God's flaming
Truth to preach, and call forth aliens to the
Shepherd's fold.   In circumvention skilled, he
Played his game full well ;—from the flock he drew
His chosen gods;—to affluence rose;—in
Char'ots swept the higher courts ;—stood first in
Fashions vile ; and in the sacred desk, with
Marble heart,—oft swelled in gaudy form, to
Rob his soul,—the liv'ry of God ; and as
Lost angels, wove his shroud of mournful dye,
To plunge the lake of sins eternal ire.
His heart is veiled no more!—the Judge has broke
His spell! and the harvest due to him shall
Now be rept in ample sheaves,—laden with
Fruit ,—such as dying spirits only share.
Had he the solar system made of gold,
And countless stars that gem the distant space ;
He'd give them all his day of grace to buy,
That hope might claim lost Paradise again.

Too late his eyes expand,—his soul takes heed !
For the door is shut ! and the false virgin
That had no oil, shall enter in no more.
   Sinners of all grades, surround the white throne !
The'swearer,—reviler,—miser,—tattler,—thief,
And all Adam's race that died in sin, have
Met in this countless throng. The Judge now reads
Their solemn sentence, " depart ye cursed
Into everlasting fire, prepared for
The devil and his angels," while saints and
Seraphim confirm the righteous verdict,
With the loud acclamations of " amen !"
   Once more I sweep my lyre in tones of woe.
Hark ! I hear the victim's wail as she sails
The flaming sea,—bound in the serpent's coil
Of baneful fangs, and tail of venomed dart.
And as he wounds her dying soul, with sting
Imbued in God's eternal ire, I hear
Her shrieks and bitter groans that chime the dirge
Of angels lost,—uttered in deep-toned wails
Through all the howling regions of the damned.
Made fast in chains of wrath, and devils' fangs,
She struggles to be free ! but strives in vain.
   On either side o'er this vast lake of fire,
I see spirit war with spirit,—demon
War with demon,—serpent coil with serpent !
And onward sweep in combat sore ! dying
By their wounds the sad death lost spirits die.
But in demise they live ! for spirit has
No end ! survives all life but God's ! This tells
The climax of their doom ! and buries hope,
Once free to gain, in Hell's eternal grave.
   Still gazing on this sea of fire, dire sights
I see,—dread sounds I hear. As the flaming
Pit of damnation deep expands its jaws
Of liquid fire ! throwing its curly waves
Of calid flames, and smoke of sulph'rous fumes,
O'er the deep gulf of woe ! I hear the lost
Spirit shriek, but shriek in vain ! see scalding

Tears distil, " but not in Mercy's sight!" hear
Sighs that ever sigh! groans that ever groan!
And dashing waves of endless ire in dread
Succession follow wave! and most wretched
Beings curse their birth,—the scorching flames,—the
Serpent's fangs,—his deadly coil,—their day of
Grace expired,—their father's pray'r,—their mother's
Tears,—their sister's kind reproof,—the blood of
Jesus,—the groans of Calv'ry,—the wails of
Gethsemane,—the Book of Life, and God who
Their existence gave.   Then comes a voice of
Utter woe, saying "this is eternal death!"
Thus the calid flames o'erspread the lake of
Fire, such as the lost spirit only feels.
   In what consists, and where the justice of
The sinner's doom?   What forged his chains amid
Those demons bound, and swelled those waves that roll
In endless fire?   What treason bar'd the gate
Of Heav'n,—spurned the favor of God,—kindled
His wrath,—drew scalding tears from victims lost,
And chained them fast in Hell's eternal ire?
Let Dives tell, and God his truth confirm.
His tongue was parched in flames,—for water he
Cried in vain,—no telegraph conveyed his
Admonition to those he loved on earth;—
Mercy had fled,—the second death his doom.
He looked on Time, which tells of endless weal
Or woe to ev'ry son of Adam; and
He the jewel lost!—worse! for it wove his
Last winding sheet, and made his grave in Hell.
Reflection stung his soul with guilt,—on what?
The Gospel,—the garden,—the cross,—the pray'rs
Of God's loved ones, and resurrection of
Jesus from the tomb.   All these he spurned,—rushed
On in folly's path,—despised the blood of
His redemption,—the'cries of Gethsemane,
And all the mercies of the Son of God.
These are the darts that pierce his dying soul,
And tell the justice of eternal pain.

Horrible sight!—his day of grace expired!—
All Heav'n lost! Never again shall the sound
Of redemption salute his ear, with crowns
Of angels and the fruit of Life's fair Tree!
But his groans shall follow groan, as he sails
In the barque that plo'ghs the red waves of fire,
While God is Judge, and justice guards his throne
   O Jesus! take the blood-bought sinner,—shake
Him over Hell with eyes unveiled, ere the
Gangrene of death shall end his probation;
And the bolts of endless perdition, bind
Him fast in " the bottomless pit" of woe.
Let arrows dipt in blood divine pierce his
Heart, that he may die unto sin while there
Is hope in the resurrection of his
Soul,—believe in God,—live by faith,—pluck fruit
Immortal, and scale the highlands of heav'n.
If so, demons shall become his strangers,
And saints his guests amid the thrones of light!—
Hell shall lose his wails,—devils lament his
Weal, as he basks in the sunbeams of God,
And swells the anthems of the blood-washed throng.
   But the fallen sons of Adam, void of
The second birth, shall not die alone. A
Higher order of revolting ones, that
Stood first among the stars of light, in their
Creation wore an angel's crown,—played on
Golden harps,—like Gabriel and his train fed
On seraphs' food, and with cherubs' wings swept
The city of our God, shall share their doom.
For them was Hell prepared; but not for man.
Marvel O my soul! that angels in their
Creation pure,—the first born of Heav'n's sons,—
Bearing the stamp of God, and by him crowned,
Should with treason vile confirm their chains of
Everlasting death. 'Twas done! All Heav'n lost!
The door of Mercy closed! and the prince of
Darkness, with his fallen train, was bound for
The judgment day. That day has come, a world

Assemble!—the aliens of God appear!—
His flaming sword is unsheathed!—his book of
Records revealed! and the revolting stars
Of light hear his sentence, "Depart!" and with
Those tears expiring angels weep, they sink
To feed the flames of "everlasting fire!"
    At this great day of despair to the lost
Sinner, the right'ous ascend to fields of
Light. The Judge has declared their reward to
Be "life eternal!" and they now receive
It in the full glory of the upper
Temple. They are clad in the drapery
Of Heav'n,—have wings as angels,—sing the song
Of Moses and the Lamb,—walk the golden
Streets of Paradise,—triumph over the ‑
World,—pluck fruit immortal,—drink the waters
Of everlasting life,—see the purchase
Of redeeming blood,—feel pain no more, and
Shall never expire. While the lost millions
That waded through a Saviour's blood to Hell,
Utter their cries with Dives and Devils
Damned, these angelic saints shall fly through the
Midst of Heaven, saying "glory to God
In the highest," for his Son hath redeemed
Us from the "wrath that was, and is to come!"
As the mariner at sea, rocked amid
The ocean's tempest, rejoices when he
Enters the port of safety; so the saint,
After passing over the dangerous
Sea of life, gives thanks to the Captain of
Zion's ship, for his safe landing in Heav'n.
    Here stands the servant of the Lord, who once
Appeared on Mount Moriah with his son
Clothed in white,—with honored crown,—the purchase
Of that Savior, buffeted in the streets
Of the Jews. Lo the prophet, once in the
Flaming bush, has bid his grave farewell, and
Like an angel sings the song of rapture
To the Lamb; while Phar'oh, with his colleagues

Deep in art, descends to feel those flames, lit
Up by wrath divine.   Here the blest Psalmist
Stands with golden harp of angels' tune, to
Chime that song a Savior bought when on the
Cross he hung.   Isaiah the prophet of the
Lord, whose lips were touched with fire, shall sound no
More the dread alarm on Zion's walls, and
Be exposed to die; but songs seraphic
Move his soul with joy.   Stephen, the'first martyr
From our Savior's death, now reaps the harvest
Of redeeming blood,—with Paul at whose feet
The raiment lay.—inspired by light divine,
Will join to praise that King who saves from dark
Despair.   Peter whose humble heart reversed
His posture on the cross to that of his
Dear Lord's,—sealed his pardon by his blood, now
Basks in the sunbeams of celestial skies.
From Palestine's infantile vaults, where the
Mother's wail was born of dying groans, a
Cloud of innocents appear, who on the
Flight of speedy pinions, with unnumbered
Since the fall, soar aloft to mansions far
On high.   Christians of all grades now join the
Choirs above,—feast on angel's food, and chant
On golden harps their King's undying crown.
   Again I rise, and view the martyred throng,
Who sowed in tears while on the shores of Time.
They watched and prayed,—hoped and feared, mid
      foes of
Dangerous chase; who sought their blood to spill,
And take from them their well begotten crown.
But with sure " anchor, cast within the vail,"
And Captain skilled in life's revolving sea,
They braved the tempest of the faggot's flame ;—
The axe,—the rack,—the prison and the stake,
In hope of mansions in a brighter sky.
Their strife is o'er,—they died for martyrs' crowns
To die no more.   As their foes chime the dirge
Of the lost,—fast bound in " the second death,"

These loved ones rise higher, and still higher
On pinions of golden hue, to vie with
Cherubim of light, and pluck immortal
Fruit from Life's fair Tree, bought by the bloody
Sweat, and dying groans of the Son of God.
   I see another class of beings mid
This mighty throng.   Poor scavengers of earth,—
Bearing burdens of grievous kind, to gain
Their bread life's blood to feed.   But their sorrows
Have passed away,—their graves have given up
Their dead, and their souls and bodies meet to
Part no more.   In chariots, borne by steeds
Such as angels use, they sweep the streets of
Gold, mid Heav'n's tow'rs of light,—view the Temple's
Jasper walls,—the ambrosial city,—the
Seraphim of God,—the fair Tree of Life,
And all the glories free-born spirits feel.
No more with friends they part ;—no more shall grieve
To weep ; for their eyes have lost their tears mid
Cherubs' lyres, and Heaven's eternal strain.
   Again my soul takes wing,—soars up the stream
Of Time,—scans revolving ages,—surveys
Transpiring scenes; but one of wondrous
Height,—surpassing numbers to compute ! 'tis
Calvary's bleeding thief,—expiring mid
The dying pangs of the Son of God.   The
Wonder tow'rs ! for it was the last hour of
Grace when the cry " remember" was heard in
His Savior's ear,—his soul saved from the pit,
And borne on mercy's wings above the groans
Of crucifixion to the Paradise of
God.   Amazing change !   One hour with the mob
Reviling Christ !—the next an heir of grace,—
The friend of Jesus,—a native of the skies,—
A songster of Heav'n to vie with angels
In celestial strains, and swell redemption's
Anthem on the supernal hills of light.
   Once more I gaze ! and lo a choir of saints
On angels' steeds, with garments white, and harps

Of gold, pass round the throne ; and with a song
The ransomed spirits sing, give praise to Him
Who sits thereon.   These are they, who stood on
Zion's walls mid earth's revolving sea,—braved
The raging storm,—the darts of demons,—man's
Incarnate foes, and sinners warned by truth
And tears, to flee God's flaming "wrath to come."
Their joy is now complete.   Some speed in cars,
Propelled by power supreme,—decked with crowns
As blazing sons of God ;—some with wings in
Golden fusion dipt,—glitt'ring in sunbeams
As they sweep the skies.   These are they that shine
In courts of light as stars in heaven beam ;
For by their zeal the lost with angels sing.
    But these Christians have just begun to live.
Their course is onward, until they take the
Flight of Gabriel,—with him wing the ether
Seas,—measure the fields of supernal bliss,—
Scale the highlands of Heaven,—explore the
Immensity of space,—Jerusalem
Scan,—survey realms of the lost,—the serpent's
Deadly coil,—the spirit's wail,—then upward
Soar, and crop the flowers that bloom in Heav'n's
Eternal spring on the elysian fields
Of light.   The Time will come, when the infant
Soul in her progress, will have enjoyed more
Than all the angels from their creation
Down to the present hour.   And at this point
Human numbers fail to measure, she may
Stretch her wings and follow the lost spirit
Through ages of intense agony,—through
Fires sufficient to melt down revolving
Worlds, and exclaim in her onward flight, " My
Blood-bought song has just begun."   O God ! save
Us for this immortality of joy !
    In those bright realms the sons of light are free.
No more shall they distil their scalding tears,
In view of their digression from the path,
That leads from Time to Heaven's golden streets,
    38

And angels glitt'ring crowns.   No more shall their
Frail hearts in sunder break by death's strong grasp ;—
Tearing from them the objects of their choice,
And blighting hope in earth's remorseless tomb.
With them the scene of life is o'er,—their woes
Exhausted ;—their probation ended ;—their
Turmoil passed away ; and their expiring
Groans exchanged for Heaven's eternal lyres.
    Ye sons of God, from death and Hell redeemed,
Begin your endless song divine, praise the
Lord in numbers Heav'n born ! and ye holy
Angels swell the choir that surround his throne,
And the notes of glory that tell for him,
Who was and is, and shall remain the God
Of praise by all the holy throng.   Extol
Him ! for he is life,—light,—beauty,—wisdom,—
Mercy ! the uncreated, infinite
Jehovah !—the true God !—Creator and
Governor of all !—the Omnipotent,
Immutable Deity !—exhaustless
Fountain !—boundless affluence !—sustainer
Of Immortality !—the greatest good !—the
Alpha and Omega !—the all seeing,
Hearing, and knowing God ! yet not seen, heard,
Or known !—above all glory, or deepest
Thought !—proprietor of eternity !—
Bliss without origin !—glory in the
Highest !—the hope of Heav'n, and fear of Hell.
Far back of chaos he built his holy
Throne, ere the morning stars his praise began.
He laid eternity's foundation deep !—
Gave all existence !—on his golden throne
Embossed, alone he wore his crown, beaming
With light, such as eye shall not see and live.
What scales shall weigh Jehovah ? what numbers
Compute his love, or flaming wrath revealed ?
This is the being we call God,—the holy
One,—plastic Father,—our eternal All !—
The source from whence we came, and where return !—

Who made our souls,—bodies,—birds and beasts,—
 rills
And oceans,—all things created,—sustains
The universe,—holds the waves,—walks upon
The winds ;—at whose dire nod thunders obey,—
Fires enrage,—lightnings flash, and tempests howl.
 As sparks ascending from the smitten steel,
The starry worlds from our Creator flew ;
But like the dust that hovers o'er the scale,
Have those bright tapers fallen in his blast !
Vast to create, nor in destruction less
Is this our God who spans creation round.
Praise him for his attributes, ye holy
Sons of light ! and ye daughters of Zion
Tune your harps !—extol him above all kings !
Burn on Heav'n's altars fragrant incense of
Eternal love !—with hearts and voices swell
The rapture of the new-born song ! for he
Has redeemed you from the fires of Hell,—
Clothed you in garments white,—crowned your heads,
 and
Made you kings and priests of God. Sing aloud !
Let your banners float o'er lost angels' waves,
And Adam's race that died in unbelief.
Sing, O Death ! where is thy sting, where is thy
Victory Grave ! give thanks to God, who gave
You victory through Jesus Christ your Lord.
Ye angels shout ! and loudest ye redeemed !
Glory to God the Savior ! to God the
Father ! and God the Holy Ghost ! Amen.

My mongrel song must ever fail to meet
 The finer touches of the poet's lyre ;
It has no rhyme, in prose is incomplete ;
 Yet sings God's mercy, and his flaming ire.

Go and receive the critic's scourging hiss ;
 If he draws blood, thy truth shall be the same :
By thee some skeptic may ascend to bliss,
 And swell the glory of Messiah's name.

Live, if thou canst, when baneful winds shall roar,
   And tell the wonders of redeeming grace ;
Help the lost soul on faith's strong wings to soar,
   And spread that virtue which redeemed our race.

My Descant fly, ere millions more be slain
   In battle field, or in the Serpent's band ;
Then shall I feel thou wert not made in vain,
   Whether in Time, or in the spirit land.

SCENES OF MOUNT TABOR.

  What contrasts strange o'erspread our guilty world,
Noon day and night, caused by our planet whirled,
Stand less opposed than earthly scenes that pass
In sundry forms through time's reflecting glass.
Virtue and vice are walking side by side,
The pauper's hut stands near the castle's pride,
And Dives' chariot with its shining wheels,
Throws dust on Laz'rus who starvation feels.
  Illness and health in the same mansion lie,
Sorrow and gladness in one spirit vie ;
The infant's cry and dying groans arise,
While tears are falling from the mourner's eyes ;
The fun'ral throng tread closely on the heels
Of bridal parties, in their nuptial weals ;
Here joy and woe, here life and death conspire,
To fill the world with glory and with ire.
  What strange events from the same spot appear ?
Where Ind'ans lived, the panther's tread to hear,
Where forest trees with shades the lawn o'erspread,
There stands New York, its living and its dead !
Where once was Tyre, the seas exalted queen,
The surges roll, and fishermen are seen,
Their nets to cast, where lucid waters spread
Their curly waves o'er temples of the dead.

In fallen Edom is the foxes' den,
And desert sands sift o'er Palmyra's glen.
   The hooting owl, and winds of summer's night,
Make sad their notes, where palace, hall and light,
Once in their pow'r and full orbed glory shone,
Where man a God revered, and gods of stone.
In ancient Salem the vile Arab's scorn
Is seen, as Christian pilgrims walk forlorn,
With weary footsteps to their Master's grave,
To worship Him who rose a world to save.
The Muezzin's voice floats o'er the prophets' bones,
While desert winds heap sand in their sad tones,
O'er Asia's seven churches, long gone down,
Mid death of queens and kings of mortal crown.
Thus light and darkness, good and evil chase
The world's vain phantoms to their last embrace.
But lo! a form upon Mount Tabor stood,
The Frenchman's king, intensely bent on blood.
   Kleber's three thousand troops in combat sore,
Now fight, where lances play and bullets pour,
Nine times their number of a Turkish band,
Whose horse and riders bow to kiss the sand.
Their cannons' thunder make the earth to quake,
And mortal wounds the dying victims shake.
Round Kleber's square the Turkish troops appear,
But balls of cannon from the French do steer,
With death for thousands of their rushing foes,
A scene that battle carnage only knows.
From horse and riders sudden ramparts rise,
By which the Turk is trembling with surprise.
   For six long hours did this fierce battle rage,
And yet, both parties in the fight engage,
Pour'd forth their death balls in their rapid flight,
Which shut the eyes of thousands from the light!
Yet fiercer still roll'd on death's rapid car,
For on Mount Tabor sat their leading Star.
   At this melee, Napol'on's steady gaze,
Beheld his army by their cannons' blaze;
His foes, vast squadrons, with their bugles' sound!
And sabres bright, to scatter death around!
   *38

The chaos of battle spread over the plain,
Where thousands of warr'ors lay bleeding and slain.
   Napol'on now from Tabor's height descends,
His cannon's thunder news to Kleber sends,
He and his guard rush to the plains below,
And in their wrath make sanguine streams to flow—
Vanquish their foes, who in confusion flee
To Jordan's stream for life and liberty.
The slain and wounded trampled on the ground,
Cause man to weep, if man on earth is found.
   They fled! Murat was waiting for the flight,
And with his tigers fresh commenced the fight;
As lions rage they sallied on their prey,
And with their sabres drank hope's faintest ray!
No mercy showed to that ill-fated band,
Who fought to save Mahomet's promised land.
   Murat was nerved by many scenes of yore,
Which made the streets of Salem run with gore!
Which to the cross nailed fast the Son of God!
Sundered the vail,—made envy kiss the rod!
Caused the vile Jew to feel the Roman's spear,
The spurning eye to drop the scalding tear!
The Heathen's voice the Christian's God to own,
When the pure Ghost was from Christ's temple flown!
Called saints to earth from Heav'n's ample height,
To visit Tabor with celestial light,
And mandate angels to disband the tomb,
Where nature's God was held in nature's womb.
When all these scenes in Murat's mind arose,
He bowed the crescent with his bandit foes.
   Roll back my song, to ancient ages roll,
On Tabor's summit take thy seat my soul!
With eager gaze view lakes and landscapes round,
And weigh the seas of blood that stain the ground!
The sun seems bright as when at first it shone
On Kleber's men, where Turks by death were strown!
See Jordan's teeming waters wend their way,
And Naz'reth smiling in merid'an day.
'Twas on this Mount the brave Napol'on stood,
And saw beneath his soldiers wade in blood;

Where Kleber's army, but three thousand strong,
Drove from the field Mahomet's mighty throng:
But still the Sar'cen banner is unfurled,
Where once He stood, the Savior of the world.
    Again I look, and lo, how changed the scene!
There stands a man, the peaceful Nazarene,
A God incarnate, whose effulgent face
Illumes Mount Tabor with celestial grace.
With Him are three, the chosen of his love,
To whom appear two strangers from above,
Servants of God, who long before had flown,
To gather fruit hard by their Father's throne;
The friends of Him, from whom salvation came
To ancient bards that loved Messiah's name.
Mount Tabor's glory dims the human sight
Of God's disciples by supernal light!
Beneath the cloud they greatly fear and quake,
As Moses did when Sinai's Mount did shake!
They fall amazed in nature's feeble strife
With God immortal, seen by mortal life.
All terrene beauty is to them withdrawn;
No more they view Mount Carmel and the lawn;
No more behold the waves of Galilee,
'Till waning light shall make their vision free.
    From holy ones, bright shining as the sun,
On Tabor's height strange converse was begun;
Hard by the Lamb Moses the prophet spoke,
Where soon Elias in sad accents broke,
"As sent from God we on swift wings have flown,
To meet his Son with notice from his throne."
The theme rushed on,—the garden and the grave!
The sweat, the blood, the spear, the death to save.
To save a world, whose guilt creation shook,
Pure blood must spill free as the water brook.
The Son replied "My Father's will be done;
By sanguine streams the alien shall be won."
These holy agents in their flight return,
While words of fire their sainted bosoms burn;
And leave the Savior full of pensive gloom,
To wend his way through tears to Joseph's tomb.

But who is this, that superhuman shines
With Godlike grandeur in these earthly climes,
And holds sweet converse with those shining ones,
Whom angels call the Father's chosen sons?
Who, fills Mount Tabor with angelic light,
So mortal man has failed to view the sight?
That voice did tell, which from the cloud descended,
"This is my Son," before the Scene was ended.
  'Tis Mary's Son! 'tis Naz'reth's Holy One!
A God incarnate for a world undone!
'Tis he, who in the rugged manger lay,
To fill the world with songs of endless day!
'Tis he, whose sandals meager pressed the dust
Of Jewish streets, inspired with Jewish lust,
To bear his message, for salvation born,
To those lost ones, who spurned his love to scorn!
'Tis he, who stilled the waves of Galilee,
And spoke the vile and weeping sinner free!
'Tis he who bid lost demons to depart,
And fierce disease that rends the human heart!
'Tis he, who spoke and water blushed to wine,
Who raised a Laz'rus from his mortal shrine!
Who dried the tear that wet the widow's eye,
And healed the pensive mourner passing by!
'Tis he, who had not where to lay his head;
Yet made the world and raised the sleeping dead;
Whose fiat stills the ocean's bounding wave,
And saves the spirit from her gaping grave!
'Tis he, whose groans made earth's strong pillars shake
When mid-day darkness caused the earth to quake!
'Tis he, who cried upon the cross and died
Before the spear plunged deep his bleeding side.
But lo! he burst the grisly tyrant's chain!
And on Mount Zion shall forever reign.
  How wide the contrast in those objects twain,
Who stood on Tabor far above the plain:
The first a God, in human nature shown,
The next a man, whose sword the world must own;
Who spread destruction in his martial strife,
And robbed the world of glory and of life!

But no polluted touch can mar the site
Where Jesus stood in God's effulgent light.
Long shall Mount Tabor call the world to gaze
On Christ transfigured, and the battle's blaze.

ACROSTIC ON WILLIAM SHAKSPEARE.

W...here is the song confined to earth-born die,
  I..nspired with charms surpassing Shakspeare's rhyme?
L...oud sounds his harp with echoes floating high !
  L...it up by all the chequered scenes of time.

I...ngenious poet ! so by nature's light !
  A...nd more sublime by sundry springs of lore !
M...eet is thy verse, to cheer with sweet delight
  S...uch friends of time, as choose to gain no more

H...ow vain thy dramas in the halls of fate ?
  A...verse to virtue, and her shining path !
K...nowledge supernal there shuts too her gate !
  S...ecures her aliens for eternal wrath.

P...oets have sung, yet var'ous are their songs ;
  E...ach product fraught for endless weal or woe !
A... name, on dying harps to some belongs ;
  R...edemption's theme on other harps shall flow.

E...arth fledged thy fancy with its fleeting dreams '
  Thy song shall end with time's expiring flight !
Oh ! had thy numbers more of Heaven's beams !
  Thy spirit more of God's redeeming light.

CATARACT OF NIAGARA AND SUS-PENSION BRIDGE!

To the Rev. BISHOP M. SIMPSON, D.D., *of Philadelphia, Pennsylvania.*

The Wonders of Nature, made visible in Creation, confirm beyond ambiguity the existence of a Supreme Being; while Revelation proves man's responsibility to God, his immortality beyond the grave, and his eternal weal or woe.

All day, as days are counted here below,
I've ranged the banks of this myster'ous Chasm;
Whose raging voice has boomed, like thunder in
Distant tones, ever since the morning stars
Their song began. And as I gazed on the
Huge transparent mass, plunging the foaming
Gulf below, my heart was struck with fear, like
Viewing specters in the magic glass, or
Raging winds that swell the deep. And as I
Sat me down for nature to revive, sad
And fearful thoughts rushed on my soul, as I
Gazed on this phenomenon of nature's
Birth.

The king of day, was now descending
The western horizon; and ever since
The morning light had dispersed night's dreary
Mantle, my vision gazed on this direful
Cataract; producing scenes terrific
And sublime. The crystal fountains of the
Northern lakes, condensed in old Niag'ra,
With incessant sweep, near, and forever
Near the verge of this drear, and dreadful gulf!
And as they descend the vast abyss, the
Shock is heard in the distance as the voice
And proof of nature's God. Were it not for
Habit, proving no alarm, man would be

More fearful of this terrific sound, than
Of the lightning's burst in a stormy sky.
Such are the wonders of nature in this
Mighty Cascade, that the spell yet remains
Upon me; and their mementoes enchant
My spirit, and blend with my existence.

    God's hand made these mighty waters, to plunge
The deep! to shake the earth afar; and roll
On amid the gulf; ploughed by nature's stream
In solid rock, through the flight of ages.
Six thousand years this trump of God, perchance
Has sounded in the savage ear; and thus
Made known the Spirit Land. Above the Falls
The current is so strong, and suction so
Severe, the fowl can hardly rise. The red
Man, in his barque, applies the oar too late! —
His hope is lost! he to the Spirit cries!
And with a mortal groan descends the grave
Of graves. The swift-winged birds of heaven, in
Sundry plumage decked, parched by sunbeams of
The Summer's rays, bathe in vapors rising
From this foaming deep, and chant their songs to
Greet its cooling spray. Pilgrims far and near,
Rush on to view this king of Cataracts;
And by nature's incessant anthem, some
Have learned the Author of the song.

                      The dread
Mastodon of the elder world; whose tread
Made the forests shake, perchance in days of
Yore has by these waters slaked his thirst. Fierce
Armies in their pride have near this Chasm met,
With martial din, where the dying groans and
The sad echoes of the cannon's roar, were
Heard in fearful blast. The storms and tempests
Have swept around it; and the lightning's flash,
And bolts of thunder, have shook the heavens
Above; yet these waters rush on with their

Eternal song, from nature's golden harp.
This music still salutes the ravished ear,
With strains that blend amid the raging storm.

Near two miles below this Chasm is seen the
Iron Bridge,— the wonder of art,— sustained
By bolts and bars, posts and rails, gigantic
Cables, and sundry fixtures; fastened to
The iron-bound shores of two nations' pride,
O'er which the lion and the eagle soar.
On this suspended structure is seen the
Iron horse of rav'nous maw inspired with
Wood and fire, passing and repassing with
His gorgeous trains, journeying East and West
On their rushing pinions; bearing mankind
And nature's golden products, far and near.
Four iron cables, made of wiery braid,
Vast in their size, and strong with curly strands,
Extend from shore to shore, and terminate
With fast'nings, secured in solid rock more
Than twelve score feet above the river's base.
Eight hundred tons comprise the weight of this
Gigantic Bridge; twenty-four feet its width; —
Eight hundred feet its length; and the strength of
Its vast cables twelve thousand tons will bear.
Hard by this structure, on each tow'ring bank
Man's frightful vision views the turbid stream
Of raging waters, rolling and tumbling
O'er their rocky base, to plunge the distant
Lake below.   Immortal be the artist's
Name that framed and bound this gorgeous Bridge o'er
The dread Niag'ra, with light and knowledge
Drawn from the funds of the great Supreme.

Amazing magnificence is seen in
The dire waters of this mighty Cascade.
But this is a more point in the wonders
Of nature.   The forest green, waving in

The gale; the birds with plumage decked, beaming
In the sun; earth's millions of flow'rs kissed by
The dews of heaven; the swift winged clouds on which
The beauties of earth and sky commingle;
The Summer's sun glowing like the gate of
Paradise; the tow'ring mountain, on whose
Summit remains eternal snow; the vast
Prairies lit up by sunbeams waving in
The gale; the flowing rivers, mountain born,
That wend their way to kiss the briny deep;
The islands of fire that rise in the main,
And straightway are seen no more; the rushing
Tornado, with giant pinions, sweeping
Before it the groves and hamlet; and the
Oceans deep, which like clean hearts return heaven's
Image; or in their wild commotion swell
Like the heaving breasts of lions chained in
Agony; *all* combine in nature's book,
To tell the matchless glory of a God.

  If in this nether world our Father speaks
Terrible and sublime, how do the stars
Above, floating the heavens like islands of
Fire, proclaim his greatness?   How tells the vast
Blazonry of the great Original,
Which adorns the supernal fields of space
With beauty, far surpassing the diamond
Points of the mosaic texture?   If when
We look upon this Cataract, we are
Called to admiration, how much more, when
We gaze on the blue arch of heaven's
Magnificence, besieged by God's flaming
Seraphim, who keep their watch eternal.

THE AMERICAN REBELLION.

To the Hon. Poet, HENRY W. LONGFELLOW, *of Boston, Massachusetts.*

The following Poem, written January 1865, gives a brief description of some of the most prominent Battles:—the Causes and Results of the War;—its baneful Influence, on the Morals of our Nation; and the intolerable Debt, which will weigh us down like an anchor for many years.

The British Lion with gigantic power,
Once held our nation in his mighty grasp;
Sailed our broad coasts with ships and sailors brave;
Spread his fair flag o'er rivers, gulfs and seas;
And plowed the ocean in its broad domain.
But offence was given by the English crown;
Burdens were laid too grievous to be borne:
We spurned the act; and in our weakness rose
To burst the chains of despots on our shores.
Had England hushed the tempest to a calm
By her concession; and allayed our wrath,
Us she could have held; and for aught we know
Her flag might still be floating our domain.
But no kind news was whispered in our ears:
The Lion roared, his fiery eye-balls glared
To blast our hope, and force us back again.
They thought the race to conquer would be short;
Therefore they spurned concession's better plan;
Denied their guilt, their innocence proclaimed;
And thought the scheme of subjugation sure.
But hope its anchor lost! the morning bright
The evening tempest brought! and sundered wide
The father and the son.
                              Brave Washington,
Our country's chosen one, led on the band
To face the redcoats of the British isle.
Yet still we onward pressed; our char'ots drove
Through carnage, tears and blood; trusting in God

To break our galling chains. England knew not
With all her boasted skill ; nor did we know
The great I AM, would three kingdoms join, to
Aid us in our combat soro, clip Britain's
Wings, curtail her power, break off our chains, and
Cause us as a nation to be free.   Through
Groans and death seven years we fought, our flag
Obtained, and hushed the frantic Lion's growl.
Our fathers, then as one, swore to abide by
The constitution they had made, before
That God, who set them free.   The service bonds
Sealed the compact North and South, and by this
Compact, our Flag to the breeze was thrown o'er
These Western shores, to bind, or free the slave,
As the true canvass of each State should tell.
　　More than four thousand years has slavery lived
In all its forms; has been approved of God,
And by his only Son.   Through ev'ry age
Has oft been justified by church and state ;
By some approved, by some as wise condemned.
The mandate of holy sons inspired, is
"Servants their masters to obey ;" and the
Master to treat his servants as he ought,
With single eye to God as Ruler of
The whole.   When man discards these rules of right
Of sin he a servant is, and spurns the
Mandate of the Holy One, opposes truth,
And runs in sin to scourge his guilty soul.
To curse a master if he own a slave,
And say he has no Gospel claim to Heaven,
Is folly's blast, and proves a man to be
A bigot in extreme, or in his speech
A fool.   As bright a saint as ever sung
In Heaven, had bondmen in his charge.   As vile
A wretch as ever sunk to Hell, never
A servant held, or raised a master's scourge.
Like England in her provocation vile,
Some men declare their hearts from sin are free,
While rushing on in folly's vicious path
To fan those flames that scourge a stricken world.

Rebellion second in full blast has come;
Makes our vile nation to her center quake,
And feel the danger of approaching doom.
From whence these yells of woe?   Why brother slay
His brother, father his son, and son his
Father? Whence came these sanguine streams of blood?
Whence those abortive graves of flesh and bones to
Manure Virgin'a's barren soil, and give the .
Starving vultures food?   Why spreads this cloud of
Darkness o'er the land, which makes a midnight
Of meridian day?   From whence these groans
And tears, these widows' moans, and orphans' wails?
Why do the father and mother weep their
Departed son, their hope in age, the object
Of their care?   Why, a more pond'rous debt than
Ever cumbered English soil, is on our
Own to day?   Why do the hungry poor, that
Cannot dig for bread, feel the dread serpent
Fast winding his deadly coil?   Why have the
Inflated "Backs of Green," sunk beneath the
Current standard, so that fifty cents in
Gold will soon one dollar buy; which swells the
Price of all that we consume?   All this,
And vastly more, sets in upon us by
The curse of war! the most deadly evil
That ever invaded the worlds of God!
If to the extreme pursued, it would take
The life of the last man on earth but one;
And he would be the final murderer.
　　It yet remains to tell from whence this war?
Did it come to accomplish God's decrees?
Take it for granted; then call all things well;
Clear man from guilt, and charge the curse to God.
Why reason thus?   Because machines are moved
By power not their own : therefore they cannot
Answer to a charge.   If this faith be true, the
Robber has no sin; the murd'rer no guilt :
For, nothing is but what the Great First Cause
Compels to do his will   Such precepts I

Discard; but hold God's sacred Volume true.
Man can steal, or abstain from stealing; he
Can lie, or abstain from lying; he can
Kill, or abstain from killing; and thus be
Responsible for all his sundry acts.
If this be false, no sin belongs to man.
'Tis wond'rous strange that men can be so vile,
To clear mankind, and charge all sin to God,
When solemn truth to all the world declares,
Whate'er man sows he shall in harvest reap.
　　Some where belong the curses of this war.
The South condemn the North for prov'cation;
The North condemn the South for rebellion.
Suppose the North had provoked by slavery's
Limitation; the South had no right to
Rebel; but in Congress kept their seats, till
Supreme decisions made a just reply.
This would have saved our Union from the siege;
Sustained our Banner as the Nation's pride;
And bound our strength to brave the ancient world.
Conflicting strife to gain some high renown,
　　Aspiring seats of honor by self will;
A sanguine thirst that slavery must come down,
　　And freedom's voice be floating ev'ry hill,
Have caused our nation's combat, groans, and tears,
　　And stained our garments with each other's blood;
Inspired our country with her ills and fears,
　　And thronged the road that leads to Jordan's flood.
Give man his range without some just restraint;
Let him display his works of carnal will;
With brandished sword, and dirk of smitten steel,
Will stop the current of his brother's blood.
Is this the spirit that inspired the Son,
To save the thief, when on the cross he died?
　　My reader, let thy soul take wing, and with
Thy vision scan Fort Donaldson's bloody
Siege.　Behold the ramparts of our foes, their
Rifle pits of dread, their cannons breast works
Strong, sending ten thousand messengers of

Death to thin our ranks, and stain the soil with
Gore. The martial dirge begins; bay'nets clash
With bay'nets, cannon answer cannon, and
Send their charges through solid masses of
Flesh and blood, staining the earth with crimson,
And strowing it with the pulseless dead. In
That dire conflict, sabre clashed with sabre,
Blood followed blood, and thousands for the last
Time beheld the light! At last we put our
En'mies to flight, and raised our standard there.
And all for what? to crush the rebel, and
Free the slave.
           Again take wing, and light on
Shiloh's plains; view the smoke o'er hill and dale;
And Pittsburg Landing with its direful scene!
See the armies in dread array, and sad
Melee: some in flight, while the main ranks face
Their deadly foes. The combat rages; our
Posts are driven in; but hark! the iron clads,
With their booming cannon have turned the day.
The frightful shells, and sundry missiles sent
Sad news to our foes, caused them to retire,
And on the field leave thousands of the slain.
Pursue them still to Shiloh's strong retreat:
The conflict we renewed; both clenched as with
A lion's grasp; again we drove our foes,
Forced their retreat, scattered them to the four
Winds of heaven, and heard of them no more,
Till they appeared at Richmond's bloody siege.
  My countrymen, once more take wing and light
On Richmond's soil; there review the dreadful
Tragedy of that land of woe, of the
Suff'ring poor, and sorrows clothed in all their
Sundry forms, to slake the thirst of Davis
And his crew; proud rebels vile as ever
Drew a sword. Behold contagious swamps, and
Filthy streams stained with Yankees', and traitors'
Blood. See foul diseases, joined with shot and
Shell, fast quenching human life, to gorge

The carrion birds of prey.   View the largest
Host that ever met on battle field, with
Martial din, in our New World of light.   See
That cloud of aliens' wrath, dyed with treason
Foul, with madness fierce, and strong drink enraged,
Rush on with speed to quench their brother's blood.
See those traitors, with hearts imbued in Hell,
Fast rush from Richmond's towers, in haste begin
The dire assault, and strow the hill and dale
With thousands of the slain.   Hear their savage
Yells, their frantic cries, as heaps on heaps of
Both armies fall, and slake their madness with
Their vital blood.   They hushed our rage, and drove
Us from the field.   Seven days in battle, and
Retreat we passed; at last our gunboats saved
Us from the storm, and bade our foes retire.
Such were the woes of Chickahominy;
Such the disasters of that plaintive scene.
Had I an angel's pen, I could not tell
The matchless sorrows of that mortal strife.
    I might pass o'er more sanguine fields of death !
I might show the battles of Fort Henry,
Vicksburgh, and Hudson, and the New Orleans
Capture.   I might mention island number
Ten, the contest of Antietam, and the wilderness.
I might refer my reader to the scenes
Of Gettysburg, Harper's Ferry, Bull Run,
Fredericksburg, and Charleston ; the Yorktown
Siege, the Mobile forts, and Savannah ours.
But why longer dwell on these tragic scenes?
We all well know that war spreads o'er the land,
And would find means to end its blasting curse.
The North and South the remedy can see ;
But by it their salvation both disdain.
As England lost *us*, so we refuse to
Yield one inch ; we have no guilt or crime.   But
Say the South, " you have intruded on our rights,
And we will not bow."   Thus fireeaters and
Radicals keep up the war, and fan its

Flames. Suppose we conquer in the end; which
No eye can see, no tongue can tell; is force
Of arms always the better way? Is there no
Compromise to offer, to invite the
Wand'rers home? Have the South no craven knee
To sue for peace, and live?
     Had the priesthood
North and South, who the sacred altars throng;
And ev'ry political aspirant,
Pled as hard for peace as they have for war,
The bugle had never given its charge,
The roar of musketry, clangor of arms,
And messengers of death, had never been.
Too late I sing this solemn requiem!
Too late I mourn my country's fate with tears.
 Some where rests the curse of war. God will find
The culprits; for the day of reck'ning is sure,
When " he that is guilty shall be guilty
Still."
    Would to God the world possessed my faith!
Based on Gospel pillars, fanned by the spirit
Of peace, and destined to transform the world.
If so, no more human blood would stain the
Ground by the assassin's fatal blow; no
Martial din would sound; no clash of arms would
Grate upon the ear; no drum exclude the
Dying cries; no burnished arms stained with gore;
No clashing bayonets, or brandished swords;
No roar of cannon on the midnight air;
No messengers of death, sent in rapid
Flight, to plunge the victim's heart, and still the
Stream of life; no widows weep for the loss
Of them they loved; no orphans mourn for their
Fathers' sad demise; and none for murder
Make his bed in hell, or seal his doom mid
Angels lost. Then would peace sweep o'er the world,
And hush the raging of the soul to rest.
 But why the scourge of war on us to day,
Blighting our nation with its giant curse,

And rushing on in sanguine streams of woe ?
It was the frantic John Brown, the Kansas
Mob, the enraging voice of Phillips, L.
Garretson, and Smith, with ten thousand more ;
And slave contention in the Congress Hall,
That were precursors of our bloody siege.
The North provoked the South, the South rebelled :
Then bathed our nation in its tears and blood,
And sank in deeper guilt against its God.
A soothing voice might hushed the waves to calm,
And saved our country from untimely death.
Had the voice against slavery not been heard,
No war to day our brother's bones would bleach ;
No soldiers stain the Southern fields with gore.

Suppose in slavery there is human guilt,
And by vile masters evil has been done :
Does it show wisdom in a land of peace,
For this small stain to raise a mighty scourge
Of greater sin than ever slavery knew ?
That guilt, which oft has made the world to quake,
And shook the nations in their tears and blood ;
Made Rome to kiss the dust, in all her pride,
And stars of ours to darken in their gaze.
Can this be logic for our country's weal ?
Or is it madness to increase the blow ?

Methinks this war has now more evil done,
Than slavery would a thousand years to come.
Ah ! why extremely zealous for the slave ?
Is it to place the white man in his stead ?
When half of all his toil and gain, must go
To pay the debt, that makes the nation reel
And weep, before she heave her final sigh.

A murd'rer ! the vilest object of a
Fallen world ! for which crime God branded Cain ; and
For aught we know yet perpetuates the
Sable stain in all the Negro race.   Would
I be guilty of the foulest crime that
E'er inspired the heart of man ? and rob him

41

Of that boon a world " wants wealth to buy ?" worth
More to him than all the stars, or aught but
Heaven ?   More than three score years with me have
        passed
Away ; and I never slew a lamb, or
Swine ; a deer or goat ; an ox, or calf ; a
Horse, or fawn ; a bear, or fox ; and much more
Abstained from taking human life.   Be it
Still known, I don't condemn such lives to take
As these, except the priceless life of man.
Blush !   O, ye foul murd'rers blush ! that you are
The authors of the abortive departure
Of so many of the human race ; wound
Up their probation, and hastened their flight
To God ! Let not the news " reach Askelon !"
Nor strike the dread ears of the Eternal !
    O, could I lay before the human mind
The awful tragedy of war, the wails
Of suff'rers, the groans of the wounded, the
Cries of the dying, the prayers of the lost,
And flowing streams of blood ! Could I portray
To the human understanding the last
Throes of the departing spirit, as she
Bursts her clay tenement, and takes her flight
To Hell ! O, could I unfold the dreadful
Woes of the mortal strife, the bitter cries,
The scalding tears of martial sons, as they
Bid the world farewell, and wing their way to
God ! Could I describe the grave before them,
And the second death beyond, with the sad
Darkness of eternal night ! methinks I
Could transform their hearts, and bear them home to
Heaven.   But in vain the thought ! Man believes not
Till he feels the blow ! then all is lost ! yes,
Forever lost ! for his probation is
Sealed, and the long dreamless night of death in
Fearful gloom has come, where " no man can work."
Such is the climax of the warr'or's doom !
Such are the woes of his lost destiny !

Could I forever hush all martial strife,
And stay the madness of my fellow men ;
So vile assassins would no longer kill ;
But sheath their swords for universal peace,
I'd freely give all my possessions here,
And in some prison wind my mortal chain.
This would to *us* the olive branch restore,
And bring mankind to Paradise again.
This gift would be a greater boon to man,
Than all the wars of Heaven, Earth and Hell.

We stand in danger's hour, careless of our
Approaching doom. Amazed we looked upon
The English debt, surpassing kingdoms all ;
But now must weigh our own. The past four years
Have buried legions of our sons in death's
Last sleep ; and crippled myriads more, far
Beyond our computation known, to draw
Upon the public crib, with draughts to drain
Our nation, exhaust the treasury ; with
Millions of other bonds, and sundry dues.
This makes the North to feel the lash of slaves ;
And o'er her sad prostration mourn and weep.
But why in danger stand ? The Lion may
Shake his mane, gnash his teeth, and seize his prey.
France, our ancient friend, may traitor turn, the
Rebels join, to clip our wings, destroy our
Flag, and still the Eagle in his flight. No
Prophet here can tell the closing scene ; nor
Guaranty our Banner to the breeze. *Such*
May the pivot *be* on which our nation,
With all her brilliant Stars, shall sink or swim.

O, thou Great Supreme ! Thou who didst hang out
The starry lamps, revolve the Solar worlds, and
Bowled the immeasurable ocean, come
Down to this earth, and rule the hearts of men.
Still this martial commotion ; make man weep
For his treason against God and man. Bring
The North and South together on craven
Knees, with concession to heal the mighty

Breach ; and kiss each other on terms of peace.
Then by the scourge of our own hands as a
Nation vile, we will be led for pardon to
Sue, repent of sin, and return to God.
Then will our prayers for each other no
Longer be for messengers of death ; but
Peace will inspire our hearts with love to men.
Thank God ! since the following poem was
Penned, the war is ended ; the Negro freed ;
Man's blood has ceased to flow ; the sword is sheathed ;
The trumpet has failed to call men to arms ;
Bayonets cease to clash with bayonets ;
Cannon no longer roar ; the drum no more
Shall silence the dying cries ; the martial
Groans are ended ; the pulseless dead rest in
Their dreamless slumber ; and all is quiet
On the sanguine fields of death.   But for the
Ponderous debt that weighs us down like an
Anchor ; the mourners' wails ; the widows' tears ;
And orphans' bitter cries, we *could* breathe free.
How long ere nations shall learn war no more,
And the Gospel Banner reform the world ?

TIME'S DESTROYING FLIGHT.

To his Excellency the Right Hon. JOHN A. DIX *of
Albany, Governor of the State of New York.*

.The following Poem shows the ravages of Time, as he
sweeps over the World with his baneful influence ; lays low
the cities, and hamlets ; and makes man tremble before his
destroying Sythe. It should be read with a grave tone of
voice, and deep solemnity ; for it sings the mournful requiem
of the dead in dirges of no repeal.

NIGHT's dreary curtain shrouds the world ; man in
Sleep reposes ; the din of action is
Hushed to silence ; the birds of heaven have
Gone to rest ; the grazing herds that range the

Green lawn have laid them down to bathe in dews
Of heaven, and watch the morning light: the
Knell of midnight, borne on the breeze, tells of
Days and years departed, and of slaughtered
Millions that sleep by Time's destructive Flight!
Yet he moves on with his grisly form, and
Like the snow-wreath from the lofty mountain
Sweeps down his victims by his rapid car,
And clothes the world in mourning for the slain.

　　　'Tis midnight, and the moon-beams shine faintly
On ocean, hill, and valley.　Nature seems
Wrapt in silence, and heeds not the victim's
Groan, nor the warrior's tear.　The leaves are
Fast falling; the forest is naked for
The Winter's blast; and icy bridges cross
The silver streams.　A calm o'erspreads the earth!
Silence prevails.　But suddenly the wind
Is howling; inspired with a furious
Sweep, the forest bows before it : the domes
Totter; while the minarets and bastions
Tremble, as if struck by some terrible
Blow! yet Time moves on fearless of the scene
Around, as if no devastation shook
The works of nature, no pain was felt by
Man.　Lo, the sleeper rises from his couch,
Feels the scourges of the storm, and flies for
Refuge, but flies in vain; curses the day
Of existence, and in lost hope expires.

　Yet onward, and still onward Time pursues
His course.　The serf, millionaire, and forest
Ranger quail before him like falling grass.
He sways his iron sceptre o'er the world's
Empires ; under which ev'ry heart shall fear,
And ev'ry knee shall bend.　The Christian born
By the blood of Atonement, with flowers of
Eternal Spring planted in his spirit's
Nature, must succumb to this fell Tyrant ;
Imbibe the cold waters of Jordan's stream ;
Bow down under death's strong agony ; feel

The curse of Adam's fall; kiss the dust;
And wait the trump of the resurrection.
No finite power can clip his wings, or stay
His rapid flight; no evasion shun his
Wrath; no fervent prayer melt his marble heart!
So much for Adam's treason against God.
But for this! Time had never sent a groan
To suffering humanity! but the
Joys of Paradise would inspire the world,
And convert martial foes to angel bands.
Time holds his sceptre o'er this world insane;
Lays low in death all ranks of men; cuts down
The beautiful in days of youth; the sage
Of two score years quails under his mortal
Sythe, descends his pulseless bed, to wait the
Resurrection morn; the sturdy sire, grey
With years, bends o'er the grave, and straightway heaves
His final sigh; the Turk on his throne in
Full glory crowned, shall feel the curse of Time,
And in death's slumber press the tomb; the vile
Hero, who spills the blood of thousands, must
Fall beneath this fell tyrant, and know what
It is to expire; the simple ones, that
Rejoice in the dance, and gambol at night,
Shall to this monarch bow; the debauchee
Glorying in his shame, shall throw off his
Mortal garb under the influence of
This mighty Conqueror, and plunge his tomb;
The vile tipler, that takes strong drink until
He reels to and fro, and falls into the
Gutter; if he shall rise again, it will
Be for Time to drink his blood; yes 'tis by
This mighty victor the infant, slave, and
Monarch, must enter one common grave, to
Wait the burning fires of the last judgment.
Then shall Time lose his sceptre o'er the world
For the bliss and woes of immortality.
    Time made his sanguine mark in days of yore:
Exchanged the beauties of Paradise to
The dirge of lost Eden; the favor of God

To the curse of man ; drove Adam from his
Garden into the wilderness of sin ;
Doomed him with rebellion's baneful curse ; and
Stamped on his brow the woes of Death and Hell.
Time faltered not, but moved onward to the
Cities of the plain ; where righteous Lot was
Sorely vexed by sin ; and for which Abram
Plead to God in vain.   The angel with stern
Command, bade four loved ones to flee for life !
And they fled for Zoar's hill.   Scarce had they
Left the cities of the plain, when brimstone
Surcharged with fire, swept all their masses to
Untimely graves.   But Time's ravages do
Not end here.   Where is Babel's lofty tower ?
Long gone down under God's displeasure, with
All its builders, to meet the dust from whence
They rose.   Where is Babylon, Nineveh,
Tyre, Sidon, Balbec, and Solyma, the
Bliss of earth, which enclosed a Temple that
Eclipsed the world ?   And where are Athens, Greece,
And classic Rome, the fount of learning in
The days of yore ?   They have passed away by
Time's baneful wings to oblivion's grave.
Time shall reign as victor over all flesh,
Cities, and temples.   The maid and matron,
Son and sire, shall bend before him, until
The earth shall heave her final groan ! then shall
He, in the expiring ag'nies of death,
Deliver his keys into the hands of
Him, by whom he shall wail his dying sighs,
And bid the scenes of earth his last farewell.
    Time sits upon his iron throne, and sways
The sceptre of his vast domain.   He hurls
His mortal darts ; cuts down the fairest flowers,
And holds the keys of earth's common tomb.   The
Gay, the sober, the rich and poor, the saint
And seer, and all the nobles of the earth
Have felt the torments of his baneful sting,
And gone to their dreamless slumber.   The strong
Gigantic form, that seems to challenge his

Gnawing tooth, is driven like chaff before
The wind.   The warrior that flies to arms, and
Rushes to the battle field, hastens the
Wings of Time to drink his blood ; and leaves no
Laurels to grace his bones, fast bleaching on
The soil of death.   O Time ! remorseless Time !
Thy steps come silent on, surcharged with woe !
Thou giant murderer ! the fiend of man,
And his greatest dread.   No power can stay
Thy course, or make thy heart to bleed.   Thy
Track is onward, and none shall be able
To wear thy crown, and stop thy char'ot wheels.
     The proud condor of the lofty Andes
That soars on high amid the vault of heaven,
And with his pinions braves the fury of
The tornado, or wings the blue ether
Beyond the burst of lightning, or the loud
Thunder's voice, when night comes on furls his broad
Wing, and fast descends to the mountain top.
But Time desires no rest.   Night's mid darkness
Can find no chains his wings to bind.   His strong
Pinions rush over the World, producing
Revolution upon revolution,
Like the frightful visions of the night, that
Trouble the dreamers' heart.   Cities rise and
Fall like the ocean's waves.   Islands of fire
Spring up amid the mighty waters, and
Sink beneath the surges of the deep.   The
Lofty mountains with their burning craters, and
Sable cliffs have bowed to kiss the plains.   New
Kingdoms rise bound by the strength of ages ; yet
They sink like ships in the maelstrom, to be
Seen no more.   And those stars above, that gild
The azure vault, and with their gushing fires
Form the amphitheatre of heaven,
Like lamps of gold shine from their vast abyss,
Shoot from their sockets, and pass away in
The trackless void of ether.   Yet Time, the
Grave-digger, holds his stiffened reins ; winds up
The sinner's probation ; makes fast his chains,

And sweeps him down with one ruthless blow, to
Plunge the lake of fire, and wail with demons
Lost, where mercy's voice, shall never reach his
Ear.   All stern and fearless he faulters not
Amid the groans of victims, the change of
Matter, the graves of ages; but looks like
Other victors while sitting on his throne,
Regardless of the ruin he has made.

My reader pause! Time has not yet been thy
Murderer; but soon must build thy tomb.   The
Moon may wax and wane; years may revolve, ere
He shall cut thee down; yet thy destiny
Is sure.   Time shall reign triumphant o'er thrones
And dominions; earth shall to him bow.   Thy
Soul shall survive the wreck of Time.   If clad
In Divinity, God will sustain thee
When the angel shall swear, "Time shall be no
Longer."   Then shall immortality swell
Thy bosom, and Time be exchanged for Heaven;
Thy joy shall be that of angels, and thy
Golden harp chant the diadem of Life.

BURNING OF CHICAGO.

To the Hon. Mayor of Chicago, Illinois.

The Conflagration of Chicago, which transpired on the
eighth and ninth of October, 1871, should put mankind in
remembrance of the final Day of Retribution; when "the
elements shall melt with fervent heat;—the heavens roll
together as a scroll;" and the trump of the Archangel shall
call the dead to Judgment.

The vast empor'um of the West,
  With drooping wings, lies in despair!
Her lofty domes have lost their crests;
  For calid flames did triumph there!
Laid low in ashes gorgeous towers,
By fiery whirlwind's awful powers.

Their banks, their inns, and mansions fair;
　And stores of grain, with dry goods fell!
All felt the flames of burning air,
　Inspired with death, and fraught with Hell
Which razed the splendid halls of state;
Made mourning paupers of the great.

Chicago in its speed arose
　Like eagles in their rapid flight;
But sooner fire did interpose,
　And sunk it in the shades of night!
Burnt ships and cargoes with their sails;
Spread frightful groans and dying wails.

The baleful winds of burning waves,
　Did swift in their destruction run,
The cry was " help!"　No one that saves
　Did stay the flames! the work was done!
Low in the dust the city lies,
'Mid wild despair, and raging cries.

Thousands that had the bread of life,
　And homes to lay their weary heads,
And raiment, in this dreadful strife,
　Lost all their robes, and downy beds :—
The wails were frightful in their strain!
And horror held its frantic reign.

When quietude and peace were there,
　And shone in ev'ry beaming eye;
When songs of folly filled the air,
　And few did dream 'twas time to die;
Anon the scourge of death by fire
Silenced the pulse of son and sire.

The flames ascended up on high,
　Like serpent tongues of hissing sound;
With burning fury filled the sky,
　And spread destruction all around!
These are faint types of what shall be
When God shall set the Christian free!

The matron, sire, the youth and maid,
   Strove hard their precious lives to save,
While burning winds in ashes laid
   Sad numbers in their gaping grave !
Some braved the fury of the gale,
And by their courage did prevail.

The insane drunkard in his glee,
   Seemed not to heed the wild despair !
Did fail to hear the cry " to flee !"
   Did wait the wails of death to share !
The raging swearer cursed his God,
And fell beneath his scourging rod.

My God ! what scenes were witnessed there,
   When in her groans Chicago fell ?
What deep-toned wails did mourners share
   In their affright, no pen can tell !
The cripples, bound by Satan's ban,
Cried loud for help, to God and man.

The frantic female wailed her fate,
   She knew full well her hour was nigh !
She plead for aid ! but ah, too late !
   No stable calmed her bitter sigh !
While in her travail pains she cried,
Her offspring gave one shriek and died.

Such vast destruction made by fire
   Was seldom known since time begun !
The London flames, and Moscow's ire,
   Would fail to equal, both in one !
Such is the fire king's dreadful doom,
That cities slumber in the tomb.

Chicago's fame has sunk forlorn ;
   She lies beneath her burning flame !
Her grandeur, which did once adorn,
   Has lost the glory of its name !
Her lofty domes and towering spires
Have fell to feed their scourging fires.

Two hundred millions passed away
   In these destructive flames of fire !
Which cost the sweat day after day,
   Of many toiling Son and Sire !
Mechanics, with their tools applied,
This City reared; but soon it died.

The morning Sun in lustre shone
   On sixty spires of tow'ring height !
But soon they were in ashes strown
   Beneath the burning fires of night !
Fear not ! again your temples raise,
And in them sing Messiah's praise.

But few short years will pass away
   Till our Chicago shall arise ;
And sing the songs of brighter day
   Than ever cheered the mourner's eyes ;
For marts and inns, with mansions fair,
Shall rise in full-orbed glory there.

Kind precepts from the Son of God
   Survive his death ! for men arise,
To cheer the victims of his rod
   With cargos, full of rich supplies :
Thus, all that to his truth give heed
The naked clothe, the hungry feed.

This scene is but the faintest shade
   Of that which shall by God appear,
When sun and moon in darkness fade,
   And every mourner's heart shall fear !
Then vivid flames shall rend the air,
And all mankind in judgment share.

Let such as have survived the doom
   Of those who in Chicago fell,
Now seek a crown while there is room,
   And in the climes of glory dwell ;
Nor they alone, but all should rise
Where God's eternal treasure lies.

But few believe in that great day,
　When flames shall shroud our burning world!
When earth and air shall pass away,
　And planets from their orbits hurled!
When saints shall live, and sinners quail;
And justice in our God prevail.

But suddenly, as came the flood,
　Or our Chicago caught on fire,
This great terrific day of blood,
　Shall show to man God's flaming ire!
The skeptic then shall plunge his tomb,
And wail amid lost angels' doom.

Why not evade this endless woe,
　By seeking Heaven's eternal crown?
Why not to holy mansions go,
　And with the sons of God sit down?
Pure glory there shall fill the breast,
And give the freeborn spirit rest.

There God's loved ones shall never weep,
　Or rage amid the burning flame;
The love of Jesus will them keep　　　·
　In honor to his holy name;
There, ransomed saints shall ever sing
Redemption to their risen King.

How vile must be the sinner's heart,
　That fires the mansion of his friend?
The blazing torch he does impart,
　Proves him to be the blackest fiend!
He hurls his fire-brand, fraught with death,
Which stills the pulse, and stops the breath.

What chains of hell shall bind the soul
　Of him who burns to kill and steal?
What demon's spirit does control
　That heart which wears the devil's seal?
What tongue can tell how great his ire,
When doomed to death and endless fire?

42

"OUR FATHER."

To her Ladyship, the Hon. Poetess HARRIET BEECHER STOWE.

The following Ode to the Supreme Being is said to be the most sublime Poem on the Subject ever written by an American. The Divinity contained in this Hymn, claims the admiration of men; and should be announced through the world's dominions. It has long since been published in part, but this Ode contains the Author's full Edition.

O Thou celestial King! whose ample light
   Doth occupy all space, all nature guide;
Immutable through time's destroying flight;
   The true and living God;—there's none beside:
King above all Kings;—the Omnific One,
   Whom saints and angels never can explore;
Who spoke creation, and the work was done;
   This is our Father,—we this God adore.

Philosophy, in research most sublime,
   May weigh the ocean, and describe the star;
But no skill in prose, or the poet's rhyme,
   Surveys our plastic Monarch in his car.
Mysterious God! "Reason's brightest spark,"
   Kindled by light from Thee, "in vain would try"
To know thy wisdom "infinite and dark;"
   Or weigh the worlds that on thy pinions fly.

O God! from non-existence thou didst call
   "First chaos,"—then all creation,—from Thee
Eternity took its boundless name;—all
   Things created came from Thee;—harmony,
Life, light, bliss, thou art the origin;—thine
   All glory is, for thou dost yet create;
Thy vivid rays inspire all space Divine;
   Thou God of light,—sustaining Potentate.

Thy arms the boundless universe surround;
   Sustained by Thee, — "by Thee inspired with breath;"
Thou all creation in thy chains hast bound,
   And strangely sown the seeds of life and death!
As sparks ascending in the nitrous blaze,
   So sun and moon were born; stars sprung from Thee;
And as those orbs extend their fulgent rays,
   Like floods of silver I thy glory see.

Unnumbered worlds created by thy hand,
   Wind their vast courses through the blue abyss!
Adore thy power, obey thy dread command,
   Teeming with life, and all complete with bliss!
What are their names? orbs of celestial light!
   A golden multitude of brilliant streams!
Tapers of purest air,—in lustre bright!
   Supernal suns in all their splendid beams.

Just like "a drop of water in the sea,"
   In Thee all this unequalled glory's lost!
What are the starry worlds "compared to Thee?"
   And what am I to their Omnific cost?
Though my immortal spirit be arrayed
   In all the rapture of angelic thought,
'Tis but a speck when in thy balance weighed,
   Compared to Thee is but a cypher brought.

Yet I'm the essence of thy light Divine,
   Thy brilliant worlds inspire my bosom too;
And on my heart doth thy blest Spirit shine,
   As shines the sun upon the morning dew!
I live, and move, and on thy mercy fly,
   Thy matchless love unites my soul to Thee;
I ever feel thy quick'ning presence nigh,
   Which draws me on to thy Divinity.

O God! thy plastic arm did me create!
   Thou art the source of my immortal soul!
The song of angels in their high estate;
   Thy vast commission does all worlds control!

" Spirit of my spirit ! " my hope, my all !
  Who lit in me a spark, surviving death !
To wing its way, at thy loud trumpet's call,
  To realms inspired with thy pacific breath.

Thou art that God who bowled the oceans deep,
  And formed the mountains with volcanic fire !
But lo ! thy condescension deigned to weep,
  And die to save us from thy Father's ire !
Thou art that God who burst the marble tomb !
  Placed in thy side the keys of death and Hell !
Thy vict'ry stamped upon the grave her doom,
  That Adam's race might with the angels dwell.

Thou art the sole Director of my heart !
  O let my wand'ring spirit learn of Thee ;
Thy boundless mercy to my soul impart,
  Though but a speck in thy immensity !
Yet I must live, since fashioned by thy hand,
  And rank above the fallen sons of earth !
Short is my stay among this mortal band ;
  Soon I'll ascend where angels have their birth.

Infinite God ! thou didst my soul create,
  And stamp in me a spark of endless life !
O save my spirit from lost angels fate ;
  Bear it above the woes of dying strife !
Escort me on the pinions of strong faith
  O'er Jordan's waves, and help my spirit rise
Above this rolling sphere, by truth which saith,
  " Believe in God," and soar the upper skies.

Creative being is in me complete,
  Though my frail dust of lowest order sigh ;
My step is onward to an angel's seat ;
  I guide the lightnings as they madly fly !
A worm am I ! yet spirit in my flight !
  Strangely constructed by some plastic Sire,
Whose name is God,— the omnipresent light ;
  Transporting aliens to a seraph's lyre.

The stern commission of thy voice, "Be still,"
   The lightning's thunder with terrific sheen,—
The bounding ocean, and the flowing rill,
   Declare thy glory!—though a God unseen!
The strange construction of the creature man,
   All grades of life that through creation run,
Confirm thy wisdom in its God-like plan,
   And prove thy nature and thy name are one.

Thou art that God, who sympathized and wept
   With sisters mourning at their brother's tomb;
Thy voice awoke a Laz'rus, who had slept
   Four days a corse beneath the tyrant's doom!
Though my frail dust in sundry atoms fly
   On curly winds, or float the beaten strand;
Yet shall I hear thy mandate from on high,
   "Arise ye dead," and wing the Spirit Land.

Thou shalt be Father! when our pulse shall die,
   And our frail dust return to Nature's womb!
When in death-groans we heave our final sigh,
   And earth's vain pomp be buried in the tomb!
Thou shalt be Father! when the trump shall sound,
   And shake the vault of all creation's dead!
When in that hour the sons of God are found,
   And earth's vast millions leave their sleeping bed.

Thou shalt be Father! at the Judgment Day,
   When Death and Hell deliver up their prize;
And aliens lost in desperation pray,
   With sin's eternal weight of dying cries!
Thou shalt be Father! when the Savior's blood,
   Shall grace all Christians for the shining shore;
To shun the woes of sin's destructive flood,
   For seraph's crowns, where death shall be no more.

Yes, though I die, I sure shall rise again
   Amid the raging of our globe on fire;
And meet a world condemned because of sin,
   To feel the sentence of thy flaming ire!

When thou shalt sit upon thy throne, O, God !
    And call the dead around thy Judgment bar,
O let me feel thy all-sustaining nod,
    And through thy Son be safe in Zion's car.

Of thoughts unspeakable my soul is blest !
    Though feeble my perception, Lord of thee ;
Long shall thy fadeless glory fill my breast,
    And bear my "homage to thy Deity ! "
Father ! to Thee alone my thoughts can soar :
    Thou art my rock, my shield, and strong defence ;
By thy vast works thy wisdom I adore,
    And call thee Father, God, Omnipotence.

BURNING OF BOSTON.

To WM. F. WARREN, *Boston, Mass., President of Boston University.*

The great fire of Boston commenced on the 9th of November, 1872, at 7½ o'clock P. M., and raged with terrific fury for fifteen hours ; burnt over some 65 acres of land, and destroyed property to the amount of more than $80,000,000. A large portion of the business part of the city was laid in ashes, and the wailing sufferers were mournful to behold.

A deep-toned dirge inspires the breeze !
    A plaintive wail the city showers !
And mournful strains rush o'er the seas,
    From frigid zones to vales of flowers ;
And tell of Boston's frightful wail,
When burning fires did there prevail.

Angel of God ! awake my lyre !
    Inspire my muse with plaintive song ;
And winds of wrath in flaming fire,
    That fill with dread the weeping throng !
Compose my descant on this scene,
While 1 portray the burning sheen.

Fire is a monster, when unbound,
   Lays cities low in prior dust !
Takes treasures rich, that man has found,
   And sweeps away his living trust;
Makes cities poor, and serfs to mourn,
While paupers' bleeding hearts are torn.

Scarce were the waves of war allayed
   Before the element of fire,
In mournful wailings was obeyed,
   When sad Chicago felt the ire ;
From thence it wafts its dismal tale,
Till men of Boston catch the wail.

Soon as Chicago's flames expired,
   Then thunder tones came booming o'er !
Her fiery waves had just retired,
   When sin's dread nature called for more !
Then Boston sunk beneath her flames,
Where scorching winds in triumph reigns.

Here son and daughter, wife and sire,
   Cry loud for help in their melee !
While flames rush on with burning ire,
   They seek for shelter ! none they see !
The marts and pyres, a burning mass,
Which suffer no man there to pass.

Their lofty stores and dry goods fell !
   And mansions fair, all felt the flames !
The dwellers lost their homes to dwell ;
   No places show their prior names :
Gone, bed and board, to feed the dust,
With other fixtures gone to rust.

Their temple soaring far on high,
   And spire, that caught the eagle's breeze ;
And lofty domes, that reached the sky,
   With fixtures brought across the seas ;
Have sunk beneath a fiery grave,
Because there was no power to save.

Soft maidens in their virgin flowers,
　　And harlots in full gems adorned ;
And libertines from shady bowers,
　　Have by this scourge of God been warned !
And the dire raging sons for blood,
Have felt this sin-avenging flood.

A smiling lass, with prospects fair,
　　Was looking for some worthy prize ;
And a fond youth in garments rare,
　　Did soon expect their nuptial ties ;
But now their crests have flown away,
For all their funds in ashes lay.

The father, with his joyful band
　　Of wife and children, near his heart,
Ten days ago feared not the hand,
　　That fiery breakers does impart :
But suddenly the scourge did rise !
Which took his treasure by surprise.

This is to some the time of woe !
　　One day be rich and poor the next :
Thus onward through this life we go,
　　Until our barges shall be wrecked ;
Then this world's scourging fires shall die,
For weal or woe, beyond the sky.

This fire 's the largest one of late,
　　Except Chicago's burning wreck,
That ever lashed the sons of fate
　　By land, or on the burning deck !
O, may we to the same give heed,
And seek a Friend for time of need.

Ye suff'ring ones, made so by fire,
　　Who have not lost your vital breath !
Amid God's just and flaming ire,
　　He often saves the soul from death !
Hears the young ravens when they cry ;
Will feed them, ere they faint and die.

Ye mourning ones that lost your all
   Amid the Boston wreck of fate ;
Be wise, and on the Master call,
   Before the call will be too late ;
Seek the rich land where angels fly,
And blood bought treasures never die.

The rich and noble saw the flames,
   In curly grandeur reach the sky ;
But could not cheer the owner's names,
   For all their treasures there did lie :—
Torn from their domicils of grace,
Their tears imbrued each other's face.

The insane drunkard sees the flame,
   In its terrific grandeur rise ;
And wants to know from whence it came,
   To give such lustre to the skies ?
Boasts of his courage, and his might !
But may the gutter fill to-night.

'Tis strange that men can be so vile,
   To steal amid the burning loss !
And leave the starving ones no smile,
   To gaze upon the smoking dross :
Such evil has its place in man,
Who work for God's eternal ban.

The produce markets felt the scourge !
   By fiery demons were assailed :
The bankers heard the flaming dirge ;
   In their lamenting crisis quailed !
Insurance jobbers caught the wound ;
Yet some of them are safe and sound.

The business men of ev'ry grade ;
   The bone and sinew of the marts ;
Must mourn amid the dismal shade,
   And feel the load the scene imparts :
Some sink beneath the blow severe,
While others rise above their fear.

The wool and leather dealers sure,
    Met by this fire a dreadful loss;
Which must be felt, and long endure,
    For some will fail to bear the cross:
On these the price will surely rise;
Then let no vender close his eyes.

But few years since the Portland fire,
    In all its sad destruction run!
The maid and matron, son and sire,
    Amid the ruins were undone!
Prophetic sign of Boston's fate,
Where slaking engines came too late.

This city soon will rise again,
    And make her narrow streets so wide,
The rushing firemen's piercing ken,
    Can slake the flames on either side;
Can drive the fire-king from his hold,
And thus secure the shining gold.

These fires, and ills of ev'ry kind,
    Are but the consequence of sin;
The curse is laid on all mankind,
    And Adam's race are bound to win:
But death's the climax of the ban,
And he is felt by ev'ry man.

Vast riches in one day were lost!
    Some eighty millions quickly flown!
On curly flames in vapors tost;
    And on the earth in ashes strown!—
Beware! ye sons of wealth, beware!
And in eternal treasures share.

In years hard by shall mansions tower!
    And inns and stores in grandeur rise;
That man may still regale the hour,
    To cheer him mid his mournful sighs!
Enjoy these blessings here below,
That God in mercy does bestow.

Bostonians, your loss is great!
  But in your sorrows don't despair!
Your temples in a better state,
  Shall higher pierce celestial air!
And harp and harpers swell their strain
In courts below, where God shall reign.

Both life and riches here must fly!
  No treasure lives, but one in God!
Then cast your anchor up on high,
  And kiss your sin-avenging rod!
That you with angel bands may meet,
And lay your crowns at Jesus' feet.

My God! how long shall wail on wail,
  For sin and folly yet be known?
How long ere peace shall here prevail,
  And Death's last Angel shall be flown?
All ills and pains of life be o'er,
And peace shall reign for evermore?

This warning should excite us all,
  To heed the direful scourging rod!
For this is far the loudest call,
  Made to Boston'ans by their God!
Flee! flee for life! and grasp the prize!
Where Gospel treasure never dies.

O God! may I no more have calls
  To swell my numbers with the fires,
Such as laid low Chicago's walls,
  And Boston's mansions, sons and sires!—
Father withdraw thy chast'ning rod,
And help us worship Thee as God.

THE AMERICAN REPUBLIC.

LAND of the free! thrice happy land!
  Her banner floats from shore to shore,
Where the Atlantic sweeps her strand,
  And waves of broad Pacific roar.

Nurtured by her prolific breasts,
  Unnumbered pleasures daily rise;
They shine in nature's brilliant dress,
  And prove to be earth's Paradise.

Vast prairies, crowned like seas of gold,
  Lit up by sunbeams, roll afar;
And silver lakes her skies behold,
  Reflecting light from ev'ry star.

Her flowing rivers, "mountain born,"
  Descend in channels "dark and deep,"
Through dreary forests, where the fawn
  Does often from his covert leap.

Diversified with vales and hills,
  Laden with fruit on ev'ry side,
Where joys abound, and music fills,
  The floating zephyrs as they glide.

Her plenty crowns each passing year;
  While ample harvests deck the land;
Her loyal sons forestall no fear.
  Though rebels prowl with hireling band.

Father! "we thank thee for this home,"
  Where sons and daughters may be free;
Where strangers "from afar may come,"
  And hail this land of Liberty.

Upon her standard place thy seal;
  Let hamlets grow and cities rise;
Give nations yet unborn to feel
  The glories of her Paradise.

On her kind angels look with joy,
  To see the heathen fetters break,
And hostile chains no more destroy
  The choice of faith for Jesus' sake.

The Gospel banner here shall rise,
  And spread her wings from shore to shore;
While man made welcome to the skies,
  Shall fear the martyr's flame no more.

NEW YORK STATE CAPITOL.

To his Exc. the Right Hon. MILLARD FILLMORE *of Buffalo, Ex President of the United States.*

This Capitol of the Empire State, located in Albany, N. Y., will be when completed according to Draft, one of the most splendid, and expensive buildings in North America. Two thirds of the Expense of its Erection will be lost; which, with other dues as unwise, will make many tax-payers groan under their ponderous load, ere this State's Debt, and that of the United States shall be liquidated. The base of this gigantic structure covers over three acres of ground.

YE sons of Mars I pray draw near,
   Learn well the story I relate ;
For legal men in bands appear,
   And lay on us a cruel fate ;
To show their talents — have their way ;
And they by votes have gained the day.

In the convention at the Hall,
   Where senators in glory met ;
They gave at once a solemn call,
   Did representatives beset,
To broach the case in house of State,
A Capitol, sublime and great.

This rusty building, we all see,
   Can be no longer fit for use ;
It will to us a nuisance be,
   Give nothing but severe abuse ;
Thus they contended long and loud !
At last they gained the legal crowd.

What now comes on the docket first ?
   How large the site ? how high the dome ?
Some view the scene with eager thirst,
   And in their random shots they roam !
Some said five acres must be sought,
And then the ground was dearly bought.

But of what size must be the base
   Of this vast Fabric tow'ring high ?
And what must be the polished face
   Of the four walls that reach the sky ?

43

What marble blocks this Temple build,
And how shall ev'ry part be filled?

This mighty Building in its form,
    Will tax mechanics greatest skill!
Not ev'ry one that braves the storm
    Of common halls, this post can fill!
Genius must take its strongest hold,
Where giant pow'rs can be controlled.

Each marble block must have its size,
    Before it on the site appear;
And in its place each number lies,
    As marked by some wise engineer;
Thus granite stone shall men prepare,
Ere they shall this huge Temple share.

Thus, they made known their wisest course,
    To build the granite Hall of State!
Ne'er looked for funds, but knew the source,
    Where ev'ry tax-payer learned his fate;
This Temple vast must surely rise,
For we all need the giant prize.

This Capitol stands on the hill,
    West from *Broadway* street below;
Its glory swells the echo shrill
    In many songsters here below!
Her lofty dome makes churches bow,
And minor temples kiss her brow.

In this our State's erected Hall,
    I fear the senate may be sold;
The greenbacks will them loudly call,
    And show to them the love of gold!
Some in the lower house may fly,
And grasp the funds while passing by.

For one, I do regret the cost
    Of treasures for this Building paid;
Two thirds of it must all be lost!
    One third would all we need have made:
But men that often live too fast,
Sometimes exhaust the working class.

Suppose twelve million tell the tale
   Of this vast Capitol of ours!
This will oft make some voters quail,
   And go against the present powers!
But on the whole, it may be wise
To make this cruel sacrifice.

This Tower is now near half complete;
   And will in its full glory rise!
Its beauty has not yet been beat:—
   It takes the gazers by surprise!
This giant mass, in sculpture bright,
Will last when millions take their flight.

This Hall shall in her glory stand,
   And swell the honors of the State!
All temples in our Union band,
   Must run the gauntlet of their fate!
For this vast Structure, most sublime,
Will last through centuries of time.

Let not our Empire State be proud
   Of millions of her treasures gone!
But may her sons with voices loud,
   No longer swell her debt forlorn!
But in the future count the cost,
Before they are in ruin lost.

Beware of ancient Greece and Rome!
   They hushed the glory of their lay!
No one could for their sins atone,
   And thus restore their joyful day;
On baneful wings they took their flight,
And sunk beneath the shades of night.

Let this we call our Empire State,
   To all the sisters wisely show,
Though we a conflict had of late,
   We will to Wisdom's Fountain go;
Look well to morals, and reform,
That we may brave the coming storm.

Our Nation groans beneath her debt,
  And quails to bear her pond'rous load !
No earthly kingdom is beset
  With dues like ours, to thwart their road,
According to their means to pay,
Or bear the burdens of the day.

The equalizer must appear ;
  Our nation will not always groan !
Our living here is now so dear,
  No serfs like us are called to mourn !
The prices ranging mountains high,
Make some to sing, and more to sigh.

HOOSAC TUNNEL.

To the Hon. Mayor of Albany, N. Y.

THIS Tunnel in the State of Massachusetts, passes through
the main Chain of the Green Mountains ; is four miles two
hundred and five rods long ; and though some tax-payers may
suffer under its influence ; yet it will be of great utility to the
West, Albany, Boston, and other villages on the line ; lessen
the Railroad expenses ; and be for the public good : Therefore we rejoice in the prospect of its consummation. The
following stanzas were written Oct. 1st, 1873, before the
Completion of said Tunnel.

MY Muse awake ! shake off thy dust !
  From thy opacous slumber rise !
No longer in obliv'on rust ;
  But seek the aged poet's prize !
Inspire thy verse with skill and art,
And with the lab'rer share a part.

Inventions of our modern days,
  Oft cheer the village gazer's sight !
Steam engines, in their sundry ways,
  Have brought the hidden things to light !
And telegraphs, with lightning speed,
Have all appeared in time of need.

Through Hoosac Mount, near five miles long,
  A tunnel was commenced of late ;
Its base was rocky, deep and strong ;
  For man and art a hopeless fate :

Yet perseverance braves her way,
And breaks on us the light of day.

Ere long the work will be complete;
  Speak loud of labor, art and skill:
No Tunnel does with it compete,
  But that beneath Mont Cenis Hill!
Near eight miles stamp that dismal road,
Which leads both ways to man's abode.

When this vast Tunnel shall be done,
  Its fame will fly from shore to shore!
Scarcely a prize like this was won
  In modern days, or days of yore:
Then let our nation loudly cry
Thanks be to men, and God on high.

The funds invested here 'tis true
  Can't be refunded to the State;
But this should cause no one to rue,
  Or mourn the sadness of his fate;
For villes and cities shall arise,
And gain their boons of rich supplies.

The transportation then shall wane;
  A saving made of cars and coal:
Oue engine on each passing train,
  Will roll the wheels that two now roll:
No more to tug o'er mountain heights,
Or risk the scene of rapid flights.

Shout! shout ye sons of Adam's ville!
  And hail with joy the coming day:
Mechanics of the Hoosac rill
  Chant! chant your notes of sweetest lay!
For this vast Tunnel shall be born,
And drive away your hopes forlorn.

True we regret that some have died
  To bring this mighty work around;
They in the jaws of death have cried,
  And caused sad mourners to abound:
But they might all been swept away,
Had they enjoyed the light of day.

Imagine now this Tunnel through,
    With cars swift passing East and West;
And passengers their course pursue,
    While each salutes his joyful guest!
Sudden they pass the gloomy vale,
Which often makes the riders quail.

Hark! hark a voice, "daylight appears!"
    Rings through the cars with joyful sound,
Which dries at once the plaintive tears,
    And sheds its lustre all around!
Noonday breaks in upon the soul!
And wisdom does the heart control.

Thus the lone band rise from their gloom,
    And shout exemption from all fear!
They hold the vict'ry o'er the tomb,
    Until some future day appear!
From midnight darkness heaves in sight
The glory of the morning light.

This scene will make Bostonians sing,
    While men of Adams join the song;
And Albany her lay shall ring,
    With strains of joy amid the throng;
And ev'ry village on the line,
Shall glory in this scene sublime.

The wonders hid in ages past,
    By our free sons are brought to light!
May these rich boons be long to last,
    And cheer the pilgrim in his flight!
May joyful tidings still appear,
To bless our hearts, and quell our fear.

Let those that bored this mountain high,
    Which made the road a level grade,
On fame as eagle pinions fly,
    And in their glory never fade;
Be to the world a Beacon Star,
That guides the stranger from afar.

America ! thrice happy land !
   Thy sons are versed with skillful art !
Move on in one united band,
   And strive to heal each other's heart :
Revere the men this Tunnel made,
Nor let their matchless glory fade.

This mighty act will live through time ;
   Bless sons and daughters yet unborn !
Its fame will spread through ev'ry clime,
   And cheer the pilgrims, oft forlorn !
This glor'ous workmanship of art,
Shall to the world rich grace impart.

But terrene joys will soon be o'er ;
   Time's fleeting wheels bear us along !
Then may we after glory soar,
   Where crowns ambrosial swell the song !
So when we fail on earth to sing,
We'll bask in God's eternal Spring.

SCENES OF CALVARY AND JOSEPH'S TOMB.

To the Rev. Bishop E. S. JANES, *D.D., N. Y. City.*

The following Poem, written Jan. 1st, 1872, describes the
most important Events that ever occurred in the history of
man. They are the Redemption of a lost World by the Blood
of the Cross, and Jesus' Resurrection from the Tomb : which
confirm to Adam's race their restoration from the grave ; the
Crowns of Immortality, or the woes of Hell.

My muse well nigh has failed to sing ;
   My harp has all but lost its sound :
My days rush on time's rapid wing ;—
   Near seventy years my life has crowned :
Yet I once more will raise my strain
In honor of my Savior's reign.

Six thousand years have nearly flown,
   Since Adam by trangression fell ;
Which makes mankind to weep and groan,
   And urge their passage down to Hell !—

The king and beggar feel the rod,
And mourn the scourges of their God.

This death is not man's only doom;
　God's anger tells beyond the grave!
Man hears Mount Sinai's thunders boom,
　Where angels lost in darkness rave!
God's rebels must receive his ire,
With demons wail in endless fire.

But hark! a voice was heard above,
　"What arm can save mankind from death?"
The Savior fraught with burning love,
　Said "I will give my blood and breath
To rear Salvation's flag once more,
That man, though lost, may God adore."

He came, the holy Jesus came,
　Assumed our nature, flesh and blood;
He bore the Son of God by name,
　To save us from sin's raging flood;
Was in the shepherd's stable born,
And often felt the Jewish scorn.

The time by God's decree had come
　When his dear Son should cheer the world;
Should call unwary pilgrims home
　By banners of the Cross unfurled;
Should feel the curse of sin for man,
And save him from lost angel's ban.

The words that burn with endless life
　The Son of God makes known to men:—
The Jew is stained with bitter strife,
　Because he spurns the Gospel ken;
Disdains to claim the Savior's love,
His only hope for Heaven above.

Scarce three short years had passed away,
　Since Jesus raised the sleeping dead,
Ere Jews made hast to seize their prey,
　And bind him in his pulseless bed:—
They trod on Mercy, God and Heaven,
And died without their sins forgiven.

Behold he stands at Pilate's bar,
 That King who made the earth and sky;
While Jews and Romans from afar,
 On wings of mental frenzy cry,
" Take him away !— not fit to live !"
While Jesus prays, " My God forgive !"

The suff'ring Savior wends his way,
 Bearing his Cross up Calv'ry's hill;
While hellish fiends in madness pray
 That soldiers may this Jesus kill !
He on his bed of sorrow lies,
Nailed to the cross before he dies.

They rear him up with muscles torn,
 A spectacle to God and men ;
The tombs obey his cries forlorn ;
 God's vengeance does the Temple rend !—
" O Father ! why in this dark hour,
Withdraw from me thy saving power ?"

While on the rugged spikes he hung,
 By soldiers driven through his hands,
The frantic hosts of darkness sung,
 To satiate satanic bands,
Until God's anger veiled the sky ;
Which made the Jew and Gentile sigh.

Darkness for three dread hours prevailed,
 From midday till the hour of three,
The heathen sage astonished quailed,
 And marveled how such things could be ;
Cried " nature feels her dying groans ;
Or the true God of nature mourns."

The tombs sent forth their sleeping dead
 When the atoning Savior died ;
The sea was heaving on its bed
 While in the pangs of death he cried !
The earthquake thundered by its God,
To make lost aliens fear the rod.

But lo ! the Savior sleeps in death !
   Hangs pale and lifeless on the tree :
He gave to God his Spirit's breath,
   And then from dying strife was free :
Nailed Sinai's thunders to his Cross,
By which all types are naught but dross.

In this wild scene of dread despair,
   When tombs were bursting,— rocks did rend,
The Jews well knew their Lord was there ;
   Yet put to death their only Friend !—
The arm of God shall bind their chains
As long as his Messiah reigns.

What deep-toned wails were these that spread
   Their gloom o'er each disciple's heart ?
What fear inspired their souls with dread
   As they did with their Jesus part ?
The scene drew forth the scalding tear,
And filled each stricken heart with fear.

His sacred blood put out the sun,
   When he set forth his dying groan !
'Twas then the work of Hell was done ;
   And few were left his death to mourn !—
Then his disciples lost their hope,
Till in the grave his slumbers broke.

A Jewish ruler craved his Lord,
   And took him from the bloody cross ;
Embalmed him with his own accord ;
   Entombed him and sustained the loss :—
But lo ! he rose from Joseph's Tomb,
And slew the foe that sealed his doom.

His loved disciples now draw near
   The marble Tomb where Jesus lay ;
They find him not ! their spirits fear
   That foes have taken him away !
But lo ! the guard like dead men fell,
When Jesus conquered death and Hell.

If Christ has triumphed o'er the grave,
   His saints shall burst the bands of death ;
His trumpet's voice their dust shall raise,
   Inspire it with his Spirit's breath !—
No more to wail and weep for sin ;
But crowns of full Redemption win.

THE DEATH-KNELL.

To her Royal Majesty QUEEN VICTORIA, *Empress
of Great Britain.*

The following dirge should be read in mournful cadence
and accents, for its momentous call to the reader is from the
dead of the past, present and future ages. It sings the dying Requiem of all flesh ; and warns man to be ready to
meet his Victor.

   · Thou Knell of Death ! toll on !
Another corse is borne to rest,
An alien found his mother's breast,—
     Thou Knell of Death ! toll on !

     Transport the pulseless dead !
On the lone bier the victim lies ;
Extinct the lustre of his eyes,
     His mortal vision fled.

     Move on, move sadly on !
The sundry dream's of love and power,
The bliss of earth's expiring hour,
     Are gone, forever gone.

     Tread soft with footsteps light ;
The blood no more his heart shall warm,
The living spirit of that form
     In haste has took its flight.

     Look on — behold him now !
The freezing power of Jordan's wave,
The signet of the gaping grave,
     Has chained his pallid brow.

Thou Knell of Death! toll on!
Another soul salutes the band
Of angels in celestial land;—
Thou Knell of Death! toll on!

Voice of the plaintive tomb!
Millions of hearts thy notes have stirred,
Thousands of years thy summons heard,
Still, still proclaim thy doom.

" Mankind must surely die !"
Thus ominates the frightful knell,
To the lone heart, its fate to tell ;
" All Adam's race must die."

Sad tolls thy plaintive chime,
To notice the vain warrior brave,
Who fell from glory to the grave,
In all his youthful prime.

But near, ah ! still too near,
The voices of ten thousand graves,
Like the wild roar of ocean's waves,
Inspire my heart with fear.

Their call is loud and plain,
Expiring son give up thy dreams,
Thy fancied wealth, and earthly schemes,
Soon, soon will be in vain.

" From whence, and who art thou ?
True friends were once hard by thy side,
Bold hearts that gloried in their pride —
Alas ! where are they now ?

" Let madness strive no more !
The sands now tremble in thy glass,
Thy earth-born vision soon will pass,
Thy day of hope be o'er !"

But why bring back again
The prior scenes of sad regret,
Life's morning dreams remembered yet,
Stamped with the curse of sin ?

Ah ! often hast thou swept
The dormant heart strings of the breast,
And sadly waked the soul at rest,
    That long in silence slept.

The tears of youth, once fled,
And death's last pangs are brought to mind ;
The chains that bound the great and kind,
    The sire, and infant dead.

Awake them not from sleep :
From their repose no murmurs rise,
Tears cease to wet the mourners' eyes —
    Must they forever weep ?

Ye careless ones give heed !
The Knell of Death will soon appear !
Let blood Divine your spirits cheer
    In this your time of need.

Will you God's mercy spurn,
For the vain glory of this life,
Which will increase your bitter strife,
    And with lost angels burn ?

Your final groans draw nigh !
No finite power can them prolong ;
For waves of Death roll fast along,
    And claim your dying sigh !

Could I withdraw the veil !
And show mankind lost angels' woe,
As they through time in madness go,
    To join the demons' wail !

They all would flee for life !
Rush for Salvation's golden car,
To gain the Spirit land afar ;
    And shout for angels' strife.

Time flies on hasty wing !
The day of grace will soon be o'er,
When God the Son shall plead no more !
    But endless sorrows bring.

In Death your mother sleeps !
Your brother fills the dreary grave !
Your sister too ;—no power could save !—
 Your father o'er them weeps.

Ye blood-bought souls draw near ;
And in the Son of God believe,
That Death your spirits may relieve,
 When Jesus shall appear.

May I my faith recall ;
My soul ! the grave is not for thee ;
Thou from devouring worms art free,
 This prison is not all.

I view those mansions pure,
Where light dispels all mortal gloom,
Bears thee above the yawning tomb,
 Thy glory to secure.

Thou Knell of Death ! toll on !
My soul no longer feels her chains,
With God's Messiah ever reigns—
 Thou Knell of Death ! toll on !

FAREWELL TO THE OCEAN.

To the Hon. Poet GEORGE D. PRENTICE, *Louisville, Ky.*

The vast Ocean, with its threatening billows, and beauty of
its calm ; often decked in full glory by the meridian Sun,
has occupied the following Numbers in their brief delineation ;
and excited to action the Author's waning pen, to chant once
more the Ocean's vast domain, and Nature's grandeur in her
rolling waves.

Thou king of day ! from thy bright throne,
 Endow this world with flaming love !
On the blue waves let light be strown
 From thy exhaustless fount above !

In Ocean depth where all is calm,
  Where surging waves and tempests cease,
Pour thy rich boon of sunlight balm,
  And hush the main to perfect peace.

My days have passed, since youthful eyes
  Did on these rolling waters gaze;
Which fills my heart with bitter sighs,
  That I no more can see those days.
Gone ! gone ! they are forever gone !
  Yet the vast Ocean's surging wave
May cheer some other hearts forlorn,
  While I am verging to the grave.

Behold the sailor of the main
  In his frail barque to brave the gale,
Till by the billows' mortal reign,
  He sinks beneath his dying wail !
Mid bounding waves he fell to sleep;
  Hushed by the waters' briny surge !
Over his corse the angels weep !
  The Ocean sings his final dirge.

'Tis sweet to gaze upon the deep,
  And muse when first the waters rolled !
Perhaps before the sun did sweep
  The blue abyss in days of old !
The morning stars that lit the sky,
  And sung the Ocean's infant song,
With all the speed their light could fly,
  In rapid flight was borne along.

Age after age has rolled away,
  Down, down the cataracts of Time !
Yet these vast waters chant their lay
  In tones of woe, and tones sublime !
Their waves are bright as when at first
  They did the beending heavens kiss ;
As when the Holy Spirit burst
  His light on Oceans' vast abyss.

Look on ! the cloud-shades from above,
   Like islands o'er the waters sweep !—
In visions oft my soul could love
   To breast the waves, and plow the deep !
Commune with nature's song, and hear
   All night the swift-winged tempests rave !
Or gaze with wonder on each sphere,
   Reflecting likeness from the wave.

To dream amid the shades of eve
   Of Ocean flags, and coral halls,
Where cold and frosty billows heave ;
   Where a bright sunbeam seldom falls !
Must often chill the heart with fear ;
   For there few breezes bless the morn ;
And nothing lives the soul to cheer,
   But icebergs in huge mountains born.

Ocean ! to thee, I say farewell !
   Though thou didst crown my infant song :—
Hard by thy shores I loved to dwell,
   And see thy waves by millions throng !
But I ere long must pass away ;
   Old age is stamped upon my brow ;
Soon I must lose life's faintest ray,
   And to the grisly tyrant bow.

These waters, when my pulse no more
   Shall move the sanguine stream of life,
Will live, and lash their beaten shore,
   And bear the ships of dying strife !
Farewell ! the night of death draws near !
   In fearful tones the surges swell !
Nerve up my soul ! shake off thy fear !—
   Farewell, " dear Ocean, fare thee well !"

Six thousand years thy waves have rolled,
   And bore thy cargoes far and near ;
Sea Captains, with their crews untold,
   Thy bosom plowed, for ports to steer ;

But this vast fountain, made by God!
   Shall in its bounded laver dry!
For earth and Hell shall feel his rod,
   And in their burning anguish cry!

Millions have on thy bosom rode
   With flags rich floating in the breeze;
But in thy waters' dark abode
   Oft slept beneath the raging seas!
But when volcanoes fire the air
   By conflagration's burning gale,
Then shall the lost deep mourning share;
   For Gabriel's trumpet shall prevail!

This world is but one common grave,
   Which holds the billions of the dead;
But waters deep, and earth, and wave,
   Shall yield the sleepers from their bed!
Then shall the elements obey
   The dreadful mandate from on high!
Then shall the Oceans pass away,
   And Adam's race for mercy cry!

If God be true, the time will come,
   When we on earth shall have no sea!—
This will be doleful news to some;
   Yet John declares this time shall be!
Then, in each quarter of the world,
   The burning mountain's fiery flame,
Shall rend the rocks,— with vengeance hurled,
   In honor to Jehovah's name.

O! could my soul withdraw the veil,
   That hides the wonders of that Day!
When Oceans waste, and fires prevail,
   And hope shall lose her faintest ray!
O! could that scene of earth on fire,
   When mounts shall quake and lava run,
Fill this vain world with vast desire
   To seek their Father's chosen Son!

A NIGHT IN GETHSEMANE.

To the Hon. Poet WILLIAM C. BRYANT, *Massachusetts.*

He comes, the suffering son of God
    Lays by the glory of his power;
He comes to feel his Father's rod,
    And save the soul in death's dark hour!
Across the Kidron, lo he cries,
To bless the world before he dies.

At midnight's hour he bore the load,
    That bound mankind in endless death!
Amid his groans for dues we owed,
    He prayed with his pacific breath!
"O Father! let this cup pass by!"
"It cannot pass!" "My Son must die."

An angel from the Spirit Land
    Consoled the plaintive son of God!
Then, mid his cries, and fearful band
    He stilled his groans, and kissed the rod!
"Father! except thy Son shall die,
The world must with lost angels sigh."

What blood was that which stained the ground,
    To save the lost from death and Hell?
What deep-toned wails in God were found,
    That man, might with the angels dwell?
The sacrifice alone can show
The boundless love he did bestow.

His voice was heard by sons forlorn,
    "Could ye not watch with me one hour?"
"This world of sin by me was borne
    Inspired by Satan's cruel power;
Oh! had you felt for me one groan,
Ye would not left your Lord alone.

"Sleep on, sleep on, and take your rest;
    Your Master now is doomed to die;
On the cold ground his soul was blest,
    There you should heard his plaintive cry;
Should watched him in his agony,
To set a world of sinners free.

"'Tis done, the dreadful die is cast,
    Judas has sold your Savior's blood!
The band he leads are rushing fast!
    Soon I shall plunge deep Jordan's flood;"
He came, the treach'rous signal gave,
Then died to fill his spirit's grave.

The frantic mob in haste appeared,
    Drew near their King,— the Victim bound;
Led him away, his ensign reared,
    Where he in mockery was crowned;
Then by false proof was doomed to die
Mid priests and elders' raging cry.

" Farewell, farewell, Gethsemane,
    The place where I have knelt and prayed;
Have met my brethren on the knee,
    With them till midnight often stayed;
Have taught them virtue, God, and Heaven,
And plead their sins might be forgiven.

" But Kidron's stream I'll pass no more;
    My tears shall ne'er the garden wet;
My smitten heart shall upward soar,
    Where sin no more shall me beset;
Farewell, farewell my sighs and tears,
I'll rise above my midnight fears."

Ye ransomed souls, behold the scene!
    Do not forget your Savior's cries;
For through the gloom his morning sheen
    In all its grandeur shall arise!
Shall burst the seal of Joseph's tomb,
And stamp upon the grave her doom.

But lo! the Son of God appears!
    The Lamb on Calv'ry slain doth rise!
The saint of God no longer fears,
    For Christ his Savior wings the skies!
From Olive's mount he took his flight
With angel bands, to worlds of light.

At God's right hand he pleads for me,
    Points to the nails, the sweat and blood,
" Father! thy Son on Calvary
    Did wash away sin's raging flood!
Forgive! forgive!" God hears his cry!
Why then shall blood-bought sinners die?

His days of toil and strife are o'er;
    With saints redeemed he wears a crown;
His blood shall stain the cross no more
    Beneath his Father's dreadful frown!
No more shall feel the soldier's spear,
The pangs of death, and midnight fear.

Ye ransomed ones come view the sight
    When he put forth his dying cries!
And bask beneath his blazing light,
    As He with angels soared the skies!
Then, when your flesh and hearts shall fail,
Your souls shall with your God prevail.